Flyaway

Flyaway

LUCY CHRISTOPHER

Chicken House
Scholastic Inc./New York

Text copyright © 2011 by Lucy Christopher
All rights reserved. Published by Chicken House,
an imprint of Scholastic Inc., *Publishers since 1920.*
CHICKEN HOUSE, SCHOLASTIC, and associated logos are
trademarks and/or registered trademarks of Scholastic Inc.
www.scholastic.com
First published in the United Kingdom in 2010 by
Chicken House,
2 Palmer Street, Frome, Somerset BA11 1DS.
www.doublecluck.com

Library of Congress Cataloging-in-Publication Data
Christopher, Lucy.
Flyaway / Lucy Christopher.—1st American ed.
p. cm.
Summary: While her father is in the hospital, thirteen-
year-old Isla befriends Harry, the first boy to understand
her love of the outdoors, and as Harry's health fails, Isla
tries to help both him and the lone swan they see, struggling
to fly, on the lake outside Harry's window.
ISBN 978-0-545-31771-9
[1. Sick—Fiction. 2. Hospitals—Fiction. 3. Swans—
Fiction. 4. Wildlife rescue—Fiction. 5. Family life—
Fiction. 6. Fathers and daughters—Fiction.] I. Title.
PZ7.C4576Fly 2011
[Fic]—dc22
2010051425
10 9 8 7 6 5 4 3 2 1   11 12 13 14 15
Printed in the U.S.A.   23
First American edition, October 2011

The text type was set in Cochin.
The display type was set in Bickley Script.
Book design by Christopher Stengel

For all of my "flock," but especially my grandparents

The Beginning

*E*very year, Dad waits for them. He says it means the start of winter, when they arrive . . . the start of Christmas. The start of everything brilliant.

When he was a boy, he would sit with Nan and Granddad in a field near the lake behind their house . . . and wait. It was usually cold, and dark, and he says they even sat through a snowstorm once. Even then, Granddad knew when they'd arrive. Dad used to think Granddad was magical for knowing that. I can remember waiting there, too, but the memory is more like a dream than something real.

The last time we all waited together was six years ago. The winter before Nan died. The last winter the wild swans ever went to Granddad's lake.

All of us were huddled by the edge of the water, and the blankets wrapped around my shoulders smelled like dusty drawers. Nan pushed a cheese sandwich into my hand and

Granddad passed around mugs of hot chocolate. I was sleepy and still, but I kept my eyes open.

And then they came, appearing like something from a fairy tale. It was as if they'd sprung from the clouds themselves. The dawn light glinted on them . . . made them seem so white. Silver almost. Their wings set the air humming.

I still remember Dad's face as he watched them. His wide eyes. The way he bit the edge of his lip, as though he was anxious the birds might not make it. When they began to circle down to the lake, Dad leaned forward a little as if he was imagining doing the landing himself.

I loved them, even then. Just like Dad did. But they scared me, too: the way they arrived out of nowhere, and so many of them. It was as if we'd dreamt them. As if they'd come from another world.

And this year it begins like that again. With Dad excited and rapping on my door. With the swans arriving . . . and with everything changing.

*E*arly morning. It's too cold to get out of bed, but already Dad's at my door. His fingertips drumming like rain.

"Isla?" he whispers. "Coming? They're here, up at the preserve. I'm sure of it."

I force my eyes to focus on the shadows around my bed . . . desk, chair heaped with school clothes, jeans and sweater in a pile on the carpet. I hold my breath as I swing my legs out from under the blankets. Sit up. Rub my hands over my arms.

Dad knocks again.

"Yes, OK, I'm up," I hiss.

I pull on the jeans and sweater. Find the thickest socks in my drawer. Hold my breath until I'm warmer. The heat hasn't come on yet. It's too early, still dark outside. Dad creaks open the door, just a crack, but it's enough to see the wide grin on his face.

"What are you doing in there? Anyone would think you're still half asleep."

"I am."

I step toward him, touching my hair to check that it's not too tangled.

"Don't worry, you're beautiful," he whispers, already turning to go. "The birds won't care."

I go back to grab a hair band, then follow Dad down the stairs, still rubbing sleep from my eyes. We both avoid the middle step that creaks. Neither of us wants to wake up Mum or Jack. This is our time: mine and Dad's. Jack comes sometimes, when he's not playing soccer, but mostly it's just me and Dad watching them. The whoopers arrive at a new lake now, at the wetlands preserve. They have ever since that winter six years ago. No one knows why they changed.

Sometimes I hope they'll come back to Granddad's lake, but Dad says they never will. He says it's too built up and overgrown there now.

We pass the bathroom, and I think about stopping to brush my teeth, but I can feel Dad's excitement, almost as if he's fizzing beside me. He's always like this. As soon as he's up, he just wants to move. The only thing he'll ever stay still for is the birds. He grabs the thermos of coffee that's on the kitchen counter. I take a slice of bread from the bread bag, then go back and grab the whole bag in case Dad's hungry, too.

As Dad locks the house, I stamp my feet and breathe warmth onto my hands. Our front yard has turned white overnight. Frost makes the grass shimmer and turns our concrete path slick as an ice cube. I cling on to Dad's arm to get to the car. No one on our street is up yet. The place feels heavy and sleepy. Even the café on the corner is quiet. We're the only ones awake in the whole world. Us and the birds.

I turn the heat in the car all the way up. Half grin at Dad to show I'm waking up. And we're on our way.

"It's not normally this cold when they arrive," I say.

"Coldest snap in twenty years. Some people said they wouldn't come at all. But they have. They've been up north for days now."

"How do you know they'll arrive here today?"

Dad shrugs. "It just feels right."

He watches the road. I shut my eyes and try to grasp another quick moment of sleep, but I can hear Dad's fingers tapping on the steering wheel. I open my eyes again. Dad's chewing on his lip, as usual. However sure he seems, he's still nervous every year that the swans won't turn up. There are dark circles under his eyes today, making him look more tired than usual. Mum says Dad hasn't been feeling well lately: She was worried when he got sent home from work last week. But I don't know. He just looks tired to me.

He pulls onto the highway. We pass a long supermarket delivery truck with its fog lights on, then that's it. No other vehicles. The sky's getting lighter, though; already it's shifted from black to purple to gray. The hedgerows are coming into focus. I take a piece of bread from the bag at my feet and chew on it. Pass a piece to Dad. He switches off his headlights. Neither of us turns on the radio. It would ruin something, somehow. It never feels like winter until Dad and I have done this, until we've driven down these roads on this cold early morning. The car ride to the preserve is always the start of it.

Dad drives past the pylons and buildings of the steel-works, past the entrance to the new power station. He turns left into the preserve parking lot, through puddles of muddy water. We're the only ones. It's too cold and early for even the hard-core bird-watchers. No one's even been around yet to unlock the Porta-Potty. If Dad wasn't with me, it would be so creepy being here. I get out of the car and listen. There's not one single sound . . . not even the trundle of the steelworks or the distant hum of the motorway. The sky is as heavy and gray as a blanket. It feels like snow's coming.

Dad grabs the binoculars from the trunk and we get going. It doesn't take long to walk to the lakes. Down the small dirt lane beside the stream, up the short ramp where the wind hits you at full force and then between the reed beds. Dad walks fast, barely waiting for me to keep up. I'm breathing hard, and the cold air makes my throat hurt. Dad stops to pick up a crumpled candy wrapper at the side of the path, his breath hanging in the air as he bends. We listen. I can't hear the usual honks and hisses. It's silent, too silent for them. Perhaps they've decided to stay up north after all. Dad would be so disappointed. He glances up at the sky, checking. But nothing.

"You sure it's today?"

Dad nods, absently. "Has to be."

It's Dad, not Granddad, who's always right about when they'll arrive now. Always. It's weird, but if there's one thing he's never wrong about, it's this. Sometimes I think it's the only thing he's actually inherited from Granddad . . . the only thing that makes me convinced they're related. We turn the last corner before the main lake, their favorite lake. Walk the final few yards. But there are no birds at all, not even any mallards or coots. The lake is as still as stone, ripple-less. For that moment it feels like all the birds in the world have disappeared.

"I don't get it," Dad mumbles.

He shakes his head, frowns. He spins around to check the sky from all angles. I look up, too.

"Maybe we're too early?" I suggest.

Dad starts walking, away from the lake. I think about the wild whooper swans, how clever they are to cover the hundreds, maybe thousands, of miles between Iceland

and here. Perhaps this year they're too tired to fly the final bit. Maybe they've given up on this wintering ground, just like they gave up on Granddad's lake. Perhaps we'll just have to watch the mute swans instead, the swans that stay here all year round. I almost laugh when I think of Dad being excited to watch mutes. We both know they have none of the noise and the mystery that the whoopers have. None of their magic.

Dad walks down the main path, toward the river. He's looking for a better view. He holds the binoculars to his eyes, scanning. Then his body goes still as he sees something. He takes the binoculars away, squints at the sky, then looks again.

"What is it?" I ask.

"No, can't be . . ." He lets the binoculars drop and they bounce against his chest. He starts forward into a run. I'm so shocked by the expression on his face that I don't even move for a second or two, I just watch him run down the path away from me. It's not the direction where the swans normally arrive from. But he's seen something.

"What?" I shout again.

He's already too far away to answer. I run after him. I'm glancing at the sky as I go, desperately trying to find out what he's seen. I don't have time to stop and use my own binoculars. He's running toward the far end of the preserve, near the corner where the new power station is. My eyes flick over it, the concrete building with its long waste chutes. The towering electricity pylons, only put up a few months ago. Suddenly, I realize what Dad must have seen, what he might be imagining. My stomach clenches into a tight fist. And I pick up my pace and pelt after him.

I've nearly caught up with Dad when I see the swans. There are about twenty of them, fewer than usual, but they're big and definitely whoopers. They are stretched across the sky, flying swiftly in that huge V shape, their wings beating in time. They must be aiming for the main lake, whooping and trumpeting as they fly. I stop and watch them. It's something I've seen so many times, but it still gets me. The dawn light on their feathers. The soft whir of wings. The way they are so huge and gangly and yet look so graceful . . . so impossibly elegant. In that moment I always understand why Dad likes them so much.

Then Dad starts waving and screaming at them and jolts me back to the freezing cold morning.

"We have to stop them," he yells.

I peel off my coat and fling it about above my head. I jump up and down. It's no good. They're only focused on getting to the lake. They don't notice us.

"They're going to hit it," Dad says.

And I feel sick then, really truly sick, because I know he's right. In the pale light, the swans can't see the wires linking the new towers, can't see the electricity fizzing in front of them. There are no red marker balls on the wires like the town council promised, nothing to show the birds what's there. I start screaming at them.

"Go away! Get back!"

But they don't see us. Even if they did, we can't stop them.

"Isla, don't," Dad whispers. "Don't watch."

But I have to. My mouth goes dry. I let my arms drop. The swan at the front looks so determined, its head bobbing in time with the beat of its wings. The rest of the flock trust it. Dad makes a tight, strangled noise as the swans falter. They slow down, change direction a little, and I think for a second that they've seen the wires. I let out a kind of breathless laugh as their wings beat furiously to take them higher. Maybe they'll make it.

But it's too late.

I hear the sizzle of the front bird hitting the wire, even from here. It tumbles toward the ground, its head twisting in surprise. Its wings limp, feathers spinning down. I feel a pain inside me, an ache beneath my ribs. I gasp. And Dad puts his arm out and gathers me toward him. He's breathing fast, too. His whole body feels tense against me, shaking. I bury my head into his bonfire-smelling coat but still I hear the smack and sizzle as another bird hits. And then another. I hold my breath. The ache inside gets worse. Then there's screeching, loud and hoarse, as the birds warn each other away. There are other birds, joining in. A constant throb of panic and wings.

"I should have realized this would happen," Dad murmurs, his voice as shaky as I feel. "Those idiots building the pylons there, and no markers . . ."

He pulls me farther toward him, so close that for a second I think I hear his heart. I concentrate everything I have on listening for it. Anything to drown out the sound of the birds all around. *Thud-thud.* Dad's own wingbeat. A gust of wind whips across my ears and under my collar, pushing my hair across my face. Dad picks up my coat from the path where I've flung it and wraps it around my shoulders.

"Put it on," he says. "It's cold."

I look up and see that his eyes are wet.

"Is it over?"

He nods. I pull back to look up. There are no birds there now, only a few feathers clinging to the wires.

"Did they . . . how many got hit?"

Dad's holding out the coat, trying to get me to put my arms through it. "The birds at the back had enough time to fly over. It's not so bad."

I turn to look behind me. "Are they on the lake?"

Dad shakes his head, glances at the sky. "Still up there. Doubt they'll winter here now."

I shield my eyes. Far above, the black specks of swans

are flying fast toward the town, following the river. Dad's watching a single swan flying much closer to us, circling slowly around the preserve. It's a youngster, grayish and small . . . maybe a female. She's all by herself. Left behind. I can tell by the way she keeps coming closer to the ground and then circling up again that she's confused, unsure if she should land. For one crazy minute I wish that I could be up there with her, helping her fly . . . showing her where to go. Does she even realize that her flock is getting farther away with each circle she makes? Again there's that ache behind my ribs. I don't want to stop looking at her. It feels like if I do, she'll fall.

Dad starts walking toward the small lake in front of us. He's heading for the reeds below the wires, the place where the swans fell. I run forward to grab his arm.

"We have to see, Isla," he says firmly. "We might be able to save them."

I keep hold of him, even though he tries to shake me off to get to them. My eyes shift to the flattened reeds where the birds lie. I don't want to see the swans like this, grounded and broken. I want to remember them before they hit the wires, flying straight and perfectly, with the light glinting off their feathers. But I also know Dad's right. We have to save what we can.

As Dad drags me closer, I see that there are three of them.

"Only three," he says quietly. "It could have been worse."

Their white, limp bodies are floating, caught in the reeds between the path and deep water, their feathers becoming waterlogged.

Dad takes off his binoculars and gives them to me. He wades in.

"But it's freezing . . ." I start to say, before Dad's sharp glance stops my words.

He breathes in quickly as the water reaches his knees. There are patches of ice floating on the surface. I hear the squelch of his boots in the mud. He reaches the first swan, drags it toward him and turns it over.

"Dead," he says.

I watch his jaw clench. He wades farther in to the next bird and I move toward the bank.

"Let me help."

"No. It's really cold."

The first swan Dad touched drifts toward me. I bend down, reach out, and grab its wing. I tow it to me. There is a deep, red gash running across the bottom of the bird's neck, wire-sized. The feathers are singed black around it and smell strangely like burnt plastic. I touch my fingers to the bird's chest. It's still warm, but there's no heartbeat. I turn away from the bird's still, glazed eyes.

Dad is feeling the next swan. "Dead," he mutters again.

He watches my face, checking to see how upset I am, before moving on to the last bird. This one's smaller than the rest and its feathers are grayish brown. A young one, on its first migration probably. I wonder if it's related to the other young one we saw flying around the preserve. It's not fair that it's traveled so far only to crash like this at the end. Dad has to wade in almost to his hips to reach it. The wind gets stronger then, making the reeds hiss and the breath catch in my throat.

"Come out of there, Dad," I say, pulling my hair back from where it's whipping over my eyes. "It's freezing. You'll die or something."

But already he's moving back toward me, dragging the swan through the water. "Here, help me," he says.

He sticks his arms under the water's surface and lifts the bird. He steps toward the bank and I reach out. Limp, wet wings brush against me. A small hiss comes from the bird's throat. I try not to look at the burnt gash on this bird's shoulder as I shift my hands to get a better grip.

"It's alive, Isla," Dad whispers. "This one's alive."

ad carries the swan back through the preserve. I have to run to keep up. One of the swan's wings drapes over Dad's arm. It's crooked, probably broken.

"It'll die if we leave it here," he says.

The swan opens its beak as if it's going to peck Dad's arm, but it's too weak even for that. It's as though it's given up already.

"Where are you taking it?" I ask.

"A vet somewhere . . . what's open on a Sunday?"

"What about Granddad's?" I say.

Dad stops to look at me. "I don't think that's such a good idea."

"But he's on this side of town, and his vet's stuff is still in the cottage."

Dad's cheeks are flushed now from carrying the bird. He

shifts it slightly in his arms as he thinks. "He won't treat a swan."

"He fixed up his neighbor's dog last year when it got run over. He can still fix things."

"He won't want to fix this."

We reach the car. I stick my arms under the swan and help carry it so Dad can get the keys from his pocket. I can feel the dampness of the feathers even through my clothes. It's hard to hold the bird still, but it's more awkward than heavy. My face is so close. I see its eyes try to focus first on me, then on Dad. Its beak is open with its pinky-black tongue lolling to the side. I want to drip water in its mouth.

"It's not going to last, Dad," I say again. "Granddad's is the closest place."

Dad nods reluctantly as he opens the trunk. "Granddad won't like it."

He goes silent, like he always does when someone starts to talk about Granddad. He puts the seats down in the back so the bird will fit. Then he takes the swan from me and together we lay it in the trunk. Sweat beads form on Dad's forehead, which is odd because the bird isn't that heavy. And Dad's strong, maybe the strongest person I know.

"You OK?" I ask.

Dad doesn't answer, just shifts the bird's weight in my direction as we both lower it gently. I try to stretch the broken wing out. I feel all those tiny bones, barely beneath the surface. There's one sticking up where it shouldn't, almost breaking through the skin. I touch it, feel its jaggedness beneath my fingers like tiny teeth. The swan pecks me on the hand. Hard. It even draws blood. It hisses until I stop touching.

"I'm sorry," I murmur, sucking at the blood.

I turn back to Dad. He looks worse now, too. His hand is pressing against the side of the car and his head is bowed. He's breathing heavily.

"Dad?"

He waves me away. "I'm fine."

I get to his side, wait until he looks at me. I forget about the swan for a moment. Dad's face is so red and sweaty. "You were cold a moment ago," I say. "You were shivering from the water. Now you're hot."

"I'm fine," he says again.

"Should I call Mum?"

"No." He straightens up to show me he's OK, but I can see the effort of moving makes him wince. "That chap was heavy, that's all."

He smiles a little, tries to make a joke of it, but his eyes won't hold my gaze and I don't believe him. He steps toward the driver's door. I stop him from getting in. "I'm calling Mum," I say, fumbling for the phone in my pocket. "Or Granddad, he's closer. Maybe you shouldn't drive."

"I'm OK," Dad says firmly. "I can drive to Granddad's, drive home even. Stop worrying."

I keep my hand on his arm. It's the only thing I can do to stop him from getting in. "Mum said you were sick," I say quietly. "She said you were sent home from work."

"Did she?" He wipes his hand across his forehead, his eyes flicking away angrily. Then he sighs, leans back against the car to look at me. "I'm cold and wet and that thing was heavy, that's all. The quicker we get to Granddad's the better, yes? That swan's going to die otherwise."

I nod, reluctantly, as he turns to open the door. I glance around the parking lot. There's still no one else here. Suddenly, I just want to get out of there, take Dad somewhere where it's not only me around. "I'm calling Mum if you're not better soon," I say.

"Fine." He brushes my words off with a flick of his hand.

I watch every single move he makes as he gets into the car. He's frowning a little and his skin looks tight. He's trying to hide it, but he's worried, and I know why. This isn't the first time this has happened. Mum said that when Dad was chopping branches in the town park, he had chest pains then, too. That's why he was sent home early. I get into the car, still watching him. The swan in the back makes a low, hissing noise. I touch its wing, and hope we all make it safely to Granddad's.

Dad tries to smile at me as we pull out of the parking lot. "He'll be OK," he says, nodding at the swan.

But I don't know whether it's the swan or him I'm more worried about. I hold my breath all the way down the lane until we're back on the main road. There are other cars around now. More people than just me and Dad. And it's not far to Granddad's house.

I can't remember the last time I went to Granddad's. It must have been months ago, back in the summer. Dad tries to avoid Granddad in the winter, says he's too grumpy and takes longer to warm up.

The exit is only a few miles down the main road, but I watch Dad carefully all the way. He drives slowly but confidently, his skin gradually turning back to its normal color. It feels strange, pulling into Granddad's lane. The hedgerows seem so much smaller and deader than I remember. But then, it is winter. I glance at the new dairy farm that's been built right next door, the one Granddad hates so much. A cow lifts her head and watches us as we pass.

The engine strains as the tires churn through the puddles of Granddad's drive. The house is how I remember it, maybe just a little more run-down. The big tree out front is fragile-looking without its leaves and the front gate is off its hinges. No dogs come running to greet us, as they would have once. It's quiet and cold when Dad turns off the engine. Dad gets out quickly and goes around to the trunk.

"I'll take it," I say, reaching for the swan.

"I'm fine, I told you," he growls, a little angry with me now. He places his hands under the bird and lifts it up. I run ahead to get the door. There's no answer at the front, so I run around to the back. Dad follows slowly behind. I watch him, as carefully as I can, checking to see if he looks as weak as he did at the preserve. But he's better now. Strong like he normally is.

Granddad is in his sunroom, sitting in the cane chair that looks out over the fields behind his house. I turn and try and see what he's looking at. Cows . . . fields . . . I can't see his lake from here. I stand on my tiptoes and listen for the sound of swans. Maybe the flock has gone there. But Dad has caught up with me now and sees where I'm trying to look.

"Not a chance," he says. "It's too built up now for swans."

I keep standing on my tiptoes, hoping to catch a glimpse of the water, but there's too much field and too many cows in between. "The flock has to go somewhere."

Dad shakes his head. "That lake's ruined from the cows." He looks back at Granddad in the sunroom. "Get the door."

Dad's cheeks are going red again and I see the strain in his face. Granddad still hasn't noticed us, so I have to rap on the window to get his attention. His eyes open wide as he sees me, as if he's trying to work out who I am. I hear his old dog, Dig, start to growl. Granddad looks behind me, his lips pressing together as he spots Dad struggling with the swan. He takes a key from under an empty plant pot and opens the door.

"Why've you brought me this?" he says immediately.

"No hellos, then," Dad mutters.

I step forward to explain. "It flew into a power line above the wetlands preserve; we thought you could fix it."

Granddad flicks his eyes skyward. "This thing's alive?"

Dad nods at that. "It is at the moment."

Granddad turns away. "You know I don't fix swans."

I reach out and grab his arm. "Please," I say. My eyes dart to Dad's face. "Just help us carry it out to your clinic."

Granddad follows my glance and looks more carefully at Dad. Perhaps he also sees that Dad doesn't look well because all of a sudden he sighs and reaches for the swan's shoulder. The surprise registers in Dad's eyes as Granddad takes the weight of the bird and lifts it right out of Dad's arms. Granddad doesn't look down at the swan, though. He keeps glaring at Dad. I brace myself, wait for them to start arguing. They usually do, at some point.

"Not worried about my shaky hands now, then?"

Granddad murmurs. "You've got some nerve, bringing this here."

"It was Isla's idea," Dad says, nodding at me. "I was going to take it to a real vet."

I grab Granddad's arm before he can say anything else, and lead him toward the old cottage where he used to run his clinic.

"You OK with that?" I ask. But Granddad's not struggling with the weight of the bird at all. As we walk the short distance to the cottage, I glance across the fields again. There are no birds in the air. No sound of swans.

I switch on the lights in the old vet's clinic. It all looks the way I remember it, just smells different. The medical posters on the walls are turning yellow at the edges, curling up over the thumbtacks in their corners. Granddad carries the bird through what used to be the reception area and into the operating room. He lays it on the steel table. Dad follows after us a moment later, shutting Dig outside.

The smell is stronger in the operating room. It's clean-smelling and dead-smelling at the same time, as if Granddad has wiped down all the benches with the same towels he'd used to treat hurt animals. I remember the last time we were all here like this. It was a couple of years ago and Granddad's other dog, Rocky, lay between us, fur bloodied from the truck that slammed into him. His head had lolled to the side when Granddad injected the anesthetic. He'd never woken up.

Dad creaks open a window and stands near it, breathing deeply. Then he sees me watching and jerks his head toward the swan, telling me to help. So I go back to Granddad. He's running his hands over the bird's body. He shakes his head as he touches the wings. I reach out and stroke its neck, touch the wet, cold feathers.

"Can you fix him?" I ask.

Granddad doesn't answer, just keeps pressing his fingers to the swan. He stares up at Dad.

"We couldn't leave him," Dad says quietly. "He would have died there."

"He'll die anyway," Granddad says. "He's in a right mess."

I step away from the table. I don't want to believe him. But the swan's eyes are starting to close and there's a horrible gurgling noise in its throat. "You can't do anything?"

Granddad stops staring at Dad and looks at me instead. His face changes as he watches me, becomes kinder somehow.

"This bird has broken its wing quite seriously," he says. "I could try and pin it, but I suspect that his liver also burst from the impact with the water. That's why he's making that sound."

Dad turns away from the window, steps toward Granddad. "You must be able to do something," he says, staring him full in the face, his cheeks reddening. I remember how flushed and sick he looked as he leaned against the car in the preserve. I don't want it to happen again here.

"Try something," Dad whispers.

"A bullet?"

They stare each other down. The swan's leg twitches and I wonder how much pain he's really in. He's brave about it, that's for sure. When I look back at Dad, he's watching me, wanting to know if I'm about to cry, probably. But, like the swan, I'm good at being brave.

"If the bird's in pain . . . ," I say. "Maybe Granddad's right."

Granddad turns away and loads up a syringe, drawing some sort of liquid from a glass vial, then flicks the top of it. Granddad catches Dad's stare and frowns. His hands shake as he moves the needle toward the swan's neck. I expect Dad to say something, but he doesn't. I know he's thinking it, though. Granddad's hands were shaking like this when he put the anesthetic into Rocky's body, too.

"Will that kill him?" I ask.

Granddad pricks the swan's skin. "No, just makes things easier. It won't be long, though, until he . . ."

I think he wants to say more, but he's not sure how. Instead, he presses down on the syringe and the liquid glides into the bird. I watch the swan's eyes shut. The skin on its eyelids is wrinkled and slack, like the skin on the back of Granddad's hand.

Granddad slides the needle out from the bird's neck. "I'll make him a bed out there." He nods toward the room at the back of the cottage where small animals were sometimes kept overnight.

I run my hand down the broken wing. The swan doesn't flinch now. Too deep in sleep. I let Granddad turn me away from the swan and push me from the room.

Dad shuts the window with a thud. "Come on, Isla, we're going," he murmurs, grabbing me by the back of my coat.

I look around to see Granddad's face cloud over. He shakes his head, then turns abruptly away. He marches back toward the house.

Dad shrugs. "He's just a grumpy old coot. Always has been."

He walks quickly to the car. I hang back a little, wait for Granddad to sit in his cane chair by the sunroom window again, wait for him to wave good-bye to us. But Dad starts the car and I run to get in it.

Mum's waiting at the door when we get home, looking from Dad's face to me and back again.

"You had the pains again, didn't you?" She grabs Dad's shoulders and stops him from going in the house until he looks at her.

"Something like that," Dad murmurs. "But it's the swans you should worry about. Flew into the wires at the preserve."

She leads him into the kitchen, ignoring his explanation of what we did today. "That's the second time this has happened now, isn't it?" She glances over at me before lowering her voice. "You're going to the doctor first thing."

"Sure, sure." Dad brushes away her concern, catches sight of Jack in front of the TV. Jack shuffles over on the couch, making room for him, and Dad's already telling him about the swans.

"The power lines, right?" Jack asks. "No markers on the wires?"

Dad shakes his head sadly. "Swans didn't have a chance."

He flops down next to Jack and the energy seems to drain out of him immediately. He's suddenly as saggy as the couch. Mum comes over to where I'm still standing by the door, takes my head between her cool fingers.

"You all right, babe?" she asks. She's looking at me carefully. I try to force my features into a smile and reassure her. It's not me I want her to be worried about.

"I'm fine," I say. I want to tell her that Dad's not, though. I want to tell her how sick he looked at the preserve, but already she's hugging me against her fleecy zip-up and brushing her fingers through my hair.

"Pizza for lunch?"

I wince as her fingers get caught in a knot. She takes a comb from her bag and tries to brush through it. I pull away from her strokes, go upstairs, and change out of my muddy jeans. When I come back down, Dad has changed, too. He's sitting back on the couch in his track pants. I sit on the floor, lean up against his leg. Dad's still talking about the swans, trying to work out where the rest of the flock has moved on to.

"Maybe they've gone back up north," Jack suggests.

Dad's not convinced. "There are other lakes around that

part of town," he says. "Behind the factories, the hospital. The swans are still nearby."

"You can *feel* it, can you?" Jack smirks at Dad. He always makes fun of the way Dad thinks he has some sort of a psychic connection with swans.

"Yeah." Dad smiles crookedly. "I'd feel it if they went somewhere else, sure!"

Jack squawks with laughter and Dad joins in a little.

"What?" Dad protests, still smiling. "I would!"

I think about that young gray swan circling around the wetlands on her own. Would Dad also feel it if she went? Would anyone? I turn around to face him.

"Can we keep looking for the swans tomorrow after school?" I ask. "Maybe go back to the preserve?"

Dad starts to nod. But Mum's in the doorway in an instant.

"Doctor first," she growls.

Dad holds his hands up in surrender. He winks at me. "Sorry, Bird," he says. "Soon."

I turn back to the TV, rest my head against Dad's knee. It's kind of nice to hear him call me by my nickname again: Bird. He hasn't done it for ages. It's what he started calling me when I was a baby, before I had a name. He said I looked like a tiny bird, something fallen from a high place. It makes me feel small and young to hear it again.

Jack turns the volume down on the hospital drama

he's been watching to talk to Dad. I can smell the mud on the bottom of his jeans and guess that he's been playing soccer this morning. I think about last weekend when he let me and Saskia come with him. He didn't seem to mind too much, even though his friends were all there. Sometimes he's good like that. Or maybe he just felt sorry for me because he knew Saskia was leaving so soon after. Maybe Mum told him to do it.

The hospital show switches to an operation scene and I turn away from it. Instead I remember playing in Jack's soccer game, how Crowy, Jack's friend, passed the ball across to me. It felt like I could run with it forever. All the way down the field with Saskia cheering on from the side. That's what I feel like doing now, running. My mind is full of images of operations and dying swans. If I could concentrate on running instead, I'm sure I'd stop thinking about them. The faster you run, the harder it is to think. At least for me.

Dad goes back to telling Jack about how the swans hit the wires. Jack wants to know every detail . . . the smell, what got broken, how cold the water was. It makes me feel sick, listening to them talk about it. I try not to hear what Dad's saying by pressing my ear more firmly against the fabric of his track pants.

Then the phone rings. I feel Dad's leg tense when Mum answers.

"I'm sorry to hear that, Martin," I hear Mum say. "I'll let them know now."

She waits a second or two before she comes into the living room, but I already know what she's going to say. Martin is Granddad, and I can see the frown on Mum's face as she tries to work out how to tell us the news.

"It's the swan, isn't it?" I ask.

She just nods. I hear Dad sighing behind me, thumping his head back onto the couch.

"Should have taken it to a real vet," he murmurs.

*T*he rain lashes against the car as Mum drives Jack and me to school. Mum's talking quietly about Dad, telling us he needs to get tests done this week.

"They think it might be his heart," Mum says.

She keeps speaking, but I can't hear the rest above the sound of the rain.

I look down Saskia's road — or the road that used to be hers — as we pass it. The *For Sale* sign is still in front of her house. I hated helping her pack up her room last week, taking down all the silly photos of us she'd stuck to the wall. Hated watching her family drive away. I press my forehead to the cold window glass, wonder what school will be like without Saskia. She'll be up in Glasgow by now, already starting at a new school. Making new friends. Fitting in. Forgetting me. I don't want to think about it. Instead, I scan the sky. I'm looking for the swan flock, though I know they won't be flying so close to the town. We drive past the corner shop where Saskia and I used to buy gummy bears. I glance back to the sky. Saskia's migrating, too, sort of. Though she's heading north, not south, and I don't know when she'll be coming back.

Mum pulls up near the bus stop and Jack's out of the car really quickly. He runs to catch up with Crowy and Rav who are already at the school gates. I crane my neck to catch a glimpse of Crowy, but he's got his back to me and I can only see his school sweater and longish hair. Mum turns around in her seat, waits for my kiss on her cheek.

"You'll be all right without Sas," she says. "You'll make new friends, you'll see."

But I'm not so sure.

Art is first and there's an empty seat next to me where Saskia would have sat. Usually I love art because it's the only class I'm actually pretty good at, but without Saskia here it's different somehow. The boys at the back stare at me when I come in, and Mrs. Diver gives me a small, sympathetic smile. I stretch out my stuff and sketchpad over the table so no one else will sit next to me.

"We're going to keep focusing on our all-important observation skills," Mrs. Diver says.

She places pieces of fruit on everyone's desk, and we all groan. We already did still lifes last year.

"These skills will help us when it comes to your major project for the semester," she continues, "which will have to do with movement and flying."

I glance up at her then, and she places a wrinkly-looking apple on my desk.

"What's an apple got to do with flying?" I murmur.

"A solid base in observation helps with everything." She winks at me, then goes back to the pencil-sketched picture of Leonardo da Vinci that's always hanging up behind her desk. "Remember Leo?" she says. "The greatest artist that ever lived? He did thousands of studies and sketches before he ever attempted to make models. We'll find out about some of these sketches in our next lesson." She looks fondly at his old, wrinkly face, as if she were looking at a poster of her dad rather than someone she'd never met.

I go back to my apple. It has a soft brown bruise and a hole where a worm's eaten into it. It smells sweet and rotten, and it's the last thing I want to look at right now. I sketch it out really quickly.

"Try and make your picture come alive, as 3D as you can . . ." Mrs. Diver is waffling on and on, waving her arms around like she does when she gets excited.

I turn toward the window. The rain is still so heavy, and the sky is gray as concrete. I wonder where the swans go in weather like this. I think of them huddling together, heads tucked back into their feathers. I wonder if the rain's been too heavy for Dad to drive to the doctor's office.

I hear the boys at the back laughing as they talk to the new girl, Sophie, who arrived a couple of weeks ago from Australia. Saskia and I sat with her at lunch one day, so I know she's nice. But the boys are teasing her about her accent, saying something about didgeridoos and *"Crocodile" Dundee*. I suppose I should invite her to sit next to me and give her a break from them. But I don't. I don't want anyone to sit there, not yet. No one apart from Saskia. It seems wrong to have a new girl in our class already, someone to replace her. I fold my arms on the table and rest my head down onto them, and listen to the pattering of the rain against the windows. It sounds a bit like swans taking off from a lake, their webbed feet smacking against the water.

Dad's in and out of the doctor's office for most of the week, getting tests done. When I come downstairs on Saturday morning, he's already in the kitchen. I stick a couple of pieces of bread in the toaster and ask him if he's sick. But instead of telling me, he says, "Let's go to the preserve today. Find the swans, and take some photographs."

"Why photographs?"

He flashes a piece of paper at me that I have to grab from him to read. It's some official-looking letter he's typed up.

"I've written to the town council," he explains. "Told them what happened with the swans and the power lines, said that if they had just put the markers up like they'd promised, there'd be no dead birds. Now we just need photos: evidence!" He's grinning excitedly.

"But are you OK now?" I ask. "With the tests and everything . . . ?"

Dad rolls his eyes. "I don't look sick, do I?"

I shake my head slowly. Because he doesn't. Not right now when he's jumping around the kitchen, thinking up plans.

"But Mum said . . ."

Dad shrugs. "Until the doctors know what's wrong, I'm not getting worried about anything. It's probably all just a false alarm anyway."

He can see I'm still reluctant. He sighs as he leans back against the counter.

"What about if I take you to get your hair cut, after the preserve?" Dad crosses his arms and waits for my answer.

I can't help smiling. All those times when I've pleaded with Mum to take me to the hairdresser, Dad had been listening.

"Mum would kill you," I say, starting to laugh. And she would. Mum loves my hair long.

"Maybe." Dad frowns as he thinks about it. "I'll say you wanted me to take you before I go into the hospital. A special day just for us."

"The hospital?" I ignore the soft *clunk* from the toaster. "What do you mean, 'the hospital'?"

Dad reaches across to pick the toast out. He flings it onto the countertop as it burns his hands.

"Nothing serious," he says quickly. "They just want to stick a tube thing into my heart, see what's going on."

"That sounds serious."

"I'm only in for a day — a couple of hours, really." He

smiles at me, then leans forward to touch my hair. "So . . . preserve first, then haircut?"

He curls a long strand around his finger and then lets it fall back into place. I've been wanting to cut my hair forever, desperate not to look like a kid anymore. But there are other things to think about right now. I study Dad's face.

"What if something happens at the preserve?" *Like last time*, I want to add.

"What can happen?" he says. "Anyway, don't you want to find the swans?"

I nod. "Yes, but . . ."

"It's settled, then."

He picks the toast up again and tosses it toward me. I catch the two pieces, just. I dig in the fridge for the butter. I use Jack's dirty plate, avoiding the jam stains as I cut the toast into quarters. Dad reaches over my shoulder and grabs a corner.

"Hey!" I slap his hand, but he moves away before I can grab the toast back.

He grins, only a little apologetic. "We're going to find that flock today," he says. "I can *feel* it. We'll look at the preserve first. But there are other lakes we could try, too."

He crunches down loudly on the toast and I move the plate before he can get another piece. Dad does seem better today. Back to his usual self. Maybe he's right when he says it's all just a false alarm.

A few hours later, I lean back against the seat and watch the streets blur past. We zoom by the Saturday shoppers trudging around in thick coats. I lean over and turn the car's heat up a notch. I can hear Dad's stomach rumbling so I dig into my pocket and find an old peppermint candy and hand it to him.

"How do you want your hair?" Dad asks, rolling the mint around in his mouth and clinking it against his teeth. "You should get it all short and spiky. You'll be like a real bird then, Bird!"

That's exactly how I want it, spiky like a cartoon character. Something different.

"I'll call you tufted duck!" Dad laughs. "Only you won't dye it white in the middle, will you? Not like an actual tufty!"

I take my cell phone from my pocket and text Saskia to

ask what she thinks. Dad turns into the parking lot and switches the engine off. He reaches around to grab the camera from the backseat.

"Ready?"

"If you are."

There are five other cars here. So at least there'll be people around if Dad looks sick again.

We keep silent as we go up the lane, both listening for the swans. Dad watches the sky, one hand already on his binoculars. I look up, too, watching for that gray youngster we saw last time, hoping she's still around somewhere. I'm also watching Dad. But if he feels sick, he doesn't show it. I shut my eyes for the last few seconds and make a quick wish before we turn the corner and see the water.

The swans aren't there. The lake is empty apart from a couple of coots, dipping in and out.

"It was worth a try," Dad says. "We'll check the rest of the preserve as well." He half smiles, trying to hide his disappointment.

We follow the main path around, past the river and toward the corner where the power station is, aiming for the wires that the swans flew into. I remember how the birds looked as they flew toward us. Unstoppable for a second.

The reeds are still flattened where they fell. Dad goes straight up to the water's edge and starts taking photographs.

I hang back. I can already see feathers on the path. A fox must have got to the bodies before us, dragged them away to eat.

"There's a wing still here," Dad calls back to me. "You can see the burn marks from where it hit the wires. The town council will have to put markers on once they get these photos."

Dad leans over the water, pulls back some of the reeds to make a gap. I catch a glimpse of a mound of feathers. I turn away, wishing the fox could have just eaten the wing, too. Dad points the camera toward it. Then the wind changes, and I get a waft of dead swan right in my nostrils. Dad starts coughing. I go back to checking the sky for the lone gray whooper. But she's long gone. Hopefully she's found her flock by now.

Dad's quiet as we circle round a different way, following the longer trail.

"We'll keep looking for them," he says. "Maybe next weekend, after I'm out of the hospital, we can try looking somewhere else?"

"If you're feeling better."

"I'll be fine."

I follow him to the small wooded section of the preserve. Dad leans against one of the trunks to catch his breath, and I wonder if his face has turned paler than before. I lean against the next tree and press my cheek against the bark to watch him. Dad tilts his head up to look between the branches, searching for smaller birds.

"Anything?"

Dad shakes his head. "All quiet." He smiles. "No swans up there at least."

We stand there for a bit, just listening to each other breathe. I watch the way Dad's breath lingers in the air like mist and then starts to fade, disappearing like it was never there. His breathing doesn't seem heavy, not like it did last time.

"Are you worried about going into the hospital?" I ask.

"It's only for a day," he says. The trunk turns my cheek cold and damp as I wait for him to say more. Dad just pushes himself away from his tree, then stands back to look at me.

"Stop worrying," he says. "You're as bad as Mum."

I keep myself pressed against the bark, watching his chest, thinking about his heart inside not working right. I hate that Dad's not telling me what's wrong with him. It makes me feel like I'm hanging in the air like Dad's breath, waiting for something. It makes me want to take him straight back to the house. Suddenly, I don't want to be out here with Dad, all by myself.

"Let's forget the haircut for today," I say. "Mum wouldn't like it much anyway."

_W_e're driving home when they appear out of nowhere, flying in a huge arrow across the sky. Dad spots them immediately.

"Whoopers," he breathes. "Let's follow them."

We drive underneath them to find out where they're going. We lose them for a bit as they fly over fields the road doesn't cross. Dad curses.

"We'll catch up with them on the other side," he mutters.

He spins into a U-turn, races back in the other direction. He's way above the speed limit when we pass the hospital.

"Be careful, Dad," I say. But he goes even faster, his eyes darting to the side to watch them. He takes a quick left onto a rough farm track. "They're landing on that field!" he shouts.

I crane my neck to look up through the windshield. The birds are circling, starting to drop down. "Is there even a lake over there?"

"No idea!"

There's nothing pale about Dad's face now. He's almost shining with excitement. My body starts to jolt as we hit the dirt track. Dad doesn't slow down.

"We've found the flock, Isla," he says. "Maybe this is their new wintering ground."

I risk a slight grin at him, laugh at his eagerness. "You're crazy, Dad."

The car bounces and judders over the dirt road until we reach a driveway to a house. Dad stops the car by the fence. There's a stile with a footpath sign on it pointing across the field to where the swans are. Dad's out of the car before I've even taken off my seat belt.

"Come on!" he yells, grabbing the camera and shoving it in his pocket.

He's clasping the binoculars as he leaps the stile. I stumble over it, my foot getting caught on something, then run after Dad across the field. He's way ahead of me so I start sprinting. The wind seems to push me from behind. Like Dad, I want to get closer to the swans. I leap over a cow pie. Stretch my legs to go faster. But Dad's quick as lightning when he gets going. I can't catch him. There's a moment where I feel amazing, running after Dad with the sun low in the sky, watching the swans descend.

Then it happens.

Dad falls down. Right in front of me. At first I think he's

just tripped in a rabbit hole or something, but he doesn't get up. He stays there, just out of sight below a small ridge, silent.

"Dad!" I scream. "Dad!"

He doesn't even raise his hand. I really start running then. I trip over tussocks of grass and almost fall. My sneakers slip on a patch of mud. But I get to him. He's on his side, clutching his chest. His breathing's funny. And his face looks damp.

"What is it? What's happened?"

I reach for him, feel his forehead. See how wide his eyes are. He shakes his head a little, opens his mouth. He can't speak. He just gapes air at me. It's like someone is stepping on his lungs.

I grab his hand. His fingers are so cold, and bluish at the tips. They tighten around mine. I move my other hand toward his chest.

"Is it here?" I ask, touching him. "Is it your heart?"

I feel the tears in my eyes welling up, blurring my vision. I don't know what to do. I imagine his heart just below my fingers, beating too quickly. Beating right through his ribs and skin, fast enough to explode.

"What's wrong?"

Dad's head moves a little. He opens his mouth again, his eyes bulging with the effort. I feel his pockets for his phone, but only find the camera. I remember seeing his phone, on the dashboard next to mine. I stare back at his face. Try to think logically. What do you do when someone's sick like this? I pull my sweater over my head and cover his chest with it.

"I need to get help," I say.

Dad moves his head again. His face winces with the effort.

"Will you be OK if I leave you?"

His breath is heavy and rattling in his throat. I try to push him back against the grass, try to make him relax. He's still straining to look up at the sky.

"Just forget about the swans!" I almost shout it at him.

Then I run. I race across the field, the wind in my face this time. It makes my eyes stream and I stumble over a clump of grass. I leap over a log, dodge puddles. I'm running faster than I've ever run before, but it's still not fast enough.

Then I'm at the fence. I half tumble over the stile and land on my knees in the dirt. Something twinges in my leg as I get up. There's a pumping sound in my ears, a fast heartbeat in my head. I fall against the car, pull open the door. Grab the phone. Dial. My fingers can't get the right numbers. I try again. This time it works. I hear a click before the emergency services answer.

"Please," I say, breathless now. "It's my dad."

They keep me talking on the phone, tell me how to make Dad comfortable. I rush back across the field, still talking. They say the ambulance will be there soon. I try to make Dad lie still and straight, try to make him warm. Then I see the flashing lights. The paramedics are already opening the back when I get there. I'm breathing too hard from running to get the words out right, but I point to where Dad is. There's three of them. Two carrying a stretcher. One keeps asking me questions.

Words are coming out of my mouth as I answer him, but I have no idea what I'm saying. I'm pulling on his sleeve, though, urging him to hurry. Dad's eyes are still open when we get there. I was so scared they wouldn't be. They get him on the stretcher and carry him back to the ambulance. Then they're loading him inside. The guy who was asking me questions stops me from getting in after him.

"Is someone coming to get you?"

I shake my head. "You're not leaving me behind." I won't let go of his arm.

So they take me with them. I grab hold of Dad's hand. His eyes dart around the ambulance. I want to tell him he'll be OK. But I can't.

They keep Dad sitting up. One of the paramedics sticks something into Dad's arm. It goes right into his vein. Then a mask goes over Dad's face and his skin slowly gets a bit pinker. The same paramedic asks me more questions. I ignore them.

"What's happening?" I say.

He says something about a monitor, something about beeping. I don't understand. But Dad's fingers are getting a little warmer than before. I just concentrate on that.

The ambulance pulls onto the highway and is driving fast now. The siren goes on. I watch the field through the darkened windows. There are still swans flying overhead, but now it feels like they belong to a different world. Cars pull over to make room for us. I catch glimpses of people's curious faces looking up through their windshields as we pass. None of this feels real.

The ambulance swerves, makes a turn. I shut my eyes. For a second I think I'm going to be sick. Then the ambulance slows down and everything inside it clinks as it goes over a bump. The doors fling open. There's a whole team of people outside. They're waiting for us. They wheel Dad through huge doors to the hospital. No one tells me what's going on.

We go into a big open room. There are even more people here. People in white uniforms, people in blue . . . others in green. Some of them stick more things into Dad's arm. Everyone's talking at once. I try to hold on to him, but there's a lady in white grabbing me around my shoulders.

"Calm down," she's telling me, over and over. "He's going to be OK."

Dad loosens his grip on my fingers. I try to pull free of the nurse who's got hold of me, but she spins me around and makes me look at her.

"We need to leave your dad here," she says. "Come with me."

I take one last look at Dad, then let the nurse lead me to an empty room and sit me down on a dark blue sofa. There's a small table in front of me with a telephone on top. All I can smell is disinfectant. She pushes a glass of orange liquid into my hand and waits until I finally focus on her. She's trying to smile at me. One of her hands is resting on my arm and she's trying to be nice, but I don't want to be here. I just want to be with Dad.

"Take a sip," she says softly, pointing to the orange liquid.

It's too orange. Too sweet.

The nurse starts talking about Dad then, says they're

going to stabilize him. She explains everything carefully, giving me too much information.

"We've called your mum," she says. "She'll be here soon."

"How did you get the number?"

She blinks at me. "You told us."

I don't remember telling her anything. She explains why there are drips in Dad's arm, what happened in the ambulance, but I can't concentrate enough to understand. I don't know how long she stays there talking to me, but it feels like a second before Mum is suddenly in the room, and Jack, and they're both hugging me. They smother me with their questions. Mum's in tears immediately. But I can't cry now. Not really.

A doctor takes Mum out of the room to talk about Dad. I lean against Jack. It's not something I would normally do, but I'm so tired, and he doesn't pull away. I think he's trying to hold back tears, which really surprises me. I can't remember the last time I saw Jack cry. His voice sounds thin and quiet when he speaks.

"I would have totally panicked," he says, ". . . today, if it had been me there with him."

I shut my eyes. I know I can't sleep, but I want to. I just want all this to go away. I want to pretend I'm back home, lying in my bed that cold morning before the swans arrived. There's a murmuring from Mum and the doctor talking outside. A part of me doesn't want to know what they're saying.

Jack is tense, though, listening. I concentrate on the sickly sweet smell of the orange drink, the feel of the soft plastic cup in my hand.

Mum comes back in with cups of tea. I don't drink mine, but it's nice to hold something warm. Nice to get rid of the sick smell of the orange liquid, too.

"We just have to wait," she says. "They're trying to stabilize him." Her eyes are red and puffy, and her voice barely a whisper.

"Will he be OK?" I ask. I lean away from Jack to look at her.

She nods quickly. "Of course."

But she doesn't look certain.

We wait there for hours. That's how it feels anyway. Soon the three of us run out of things to talk about and just sit in silence. I can't stop thinking about Dad's face in the ambulance. The panic in his eyes. I try to think about school and the swans, and even Saskia. But nothing works. Everything goes back to Dad. Another nurse comes in and asks Mum if we want to keep waiting. Mum glances at us, waits for us to nod. Then the nurse brings more cups of tea.

Jack drinks a couple of sips, then stands. "I need to move." He raises his eyebrows at me, and I look at Mum.

"I'll hold the fort," she says. "Take your phones."

I follow Jack to the public waiting room outside. There's about twenty people there. I feel their stares immediately. I try not to gawk at a girl holding her hand up in the air, a bloodied cloth wrapped around it. There's a small huddle of people around her, talking softly. I don't want to know what they're saying, but I catch a few words anyway.

"Accident... concussion. Will he be OK?"

Jack stops beside a table of magazines and flicks through them. I dig my phone deeper into my pocket when I see the signs to switch off cell phones, and keep walking around the room. There are posters about drugs and others about washing your hands. The vending machines are only half full and all the chocolate bars are gone.

I look back at Jack before I turn into a corridor. He glances up.

"Coming?" I mouth at him.

He holds up a magazine and shakes his head. "I'll wait here," he says.

I don't know why I keep going. It just feels good to move, and I want to get away, be by myself for a moment. It feels like there's something big stuck in my throat, a huge wave that's trying to gush out. I need to sit somewhere quiet. Just me. But there are no seats in this corridor. Just wide shiny floors and pale peach walls. I almost turn back. But there's an opening up ahead. Movement.

I step out into a really busy reception area. There are shops around the sides and a café opposite. There's a screen on the wall with loads of bus times flashing up. I stand right there in the middle of it all and blink. There are people everywhere: patients in pajamas, and nurses holding coffee cups, and kids. No one seems to notice me. No one even looks at me.

I move to a semicircle of blue chairs, and sit in the one closest to a fake palm tree. The big plastic leaves hang down over my head and make me feel as if no one can ever find me. I peer out from under them to see the people sitting opposite. There's an old lady with a blanket, a man in a suit, and a boy about my age with an IV stand next to him. His hair sticks up and sideways like a spiky flame — kind of the way I want my hair to look, only his is a much nicer color. A rusty light red, like autumn. My eyes fix on it, and I'm still staring when he looks at me. I'm too out of it to look away. I see him frown, probably wondering why I'm gazing at his hair. So I close my eyes, rest my head against the plastic tree trunk, and shut him out.

I can hear movement and noise all around, snatches of conversation about medical students, a plastic bag being rustled . . . someone coughing. I let it all fade into the background. I squeeze my eyes tighter shut and wait to start crying. But the tears stay inside. I just feel numb. Kind of empty.

My chair moves as someone sits in the connecting seat beside me. I can feel whoever it is wriggling around so my chair wobbles and my head jolts against the plastic trunk. I open my eyes. I'm about to turn and glare when I register who it is.

It's the boy with the IV. He's watching me. The skin on his face is so pale, but his eyes are huge and bright and warm brown. He looks beautiful and breakable at the same time. I hope he wasn't watching me try to cry.

"Are you OK?" he asks.

I open my mouth, but no words come out.

"You seem kind of upset."

I look at him more closely. Is he someone from school? Surely I'd remember someone who looks like this.

He leans back in his seat, nods at the cluster of tables and chairs in front of the café. "I've been here awhile," he says, as if it's an explanation.

He's totally relaxed, not awkward about coming up to me at all. He seems almost bored. He's quiet as he watches the other people around us, then turns to look at the clear liquid in the IV bag, as if he's checking time by it.

"Why are you here?" he asks.

It feels like the only thing I've been doing since I got here is answer questions, so why not for him, too? "My dad's sick," I say. "He had some sort of heart attack thing."

And that's when I feel my eyes welling up. I bite down hard on my bottom lip and force myself to stare straight ahead at the hospital information desk. There's a plastic Santa on the edge of it with a little bit of tinsel around his neck. Right at that moment I want to punch it. It's too early for Christmas decorations.

The boy leans toward me. He's noticed that I'm trying not to cry. He's about to say something, I'm sure of it. His face is all scrunched up as if he's feeling sorry for me. I'm so embarrassed. I mean, I don't even know him. I swallow. Take a breath. I focus on the bag of liquid hanging from his IV stand. It looks like one of those plastic bags of water you carry goldfish in. And then, because I can't think of anything else to stop what he's about to say, I ask, "Is that attached to you?"

He shuts his mouth, frowns. It looks like he's going to say something sympathetic anyway, but instead he nods. He holds out his arm and I can see the tube that leads out from the IV stand threading up his arm and disappearing somewhere underneath his T-shirt sleeve.

"It's just saline going in," he says. "Hydration. I'll be peeing it all out in a minute."

I've no idea what he's talking about, so I just keep looking at the tube on his arm.

He moves his wrist toward me, turns it over to show me a thick hospital band fastened there. There's writing on it. *Harry Brambling.* I guess it must be his name. He looks down at me like he wants to know mine. But I'm still too flustered by all the emotions trying to rise in my throat.

"There's a bird called that . . . brambling . . . ," I say before I mean to. "They migrate from Norway." Then I feel like an idiot.

The boy, Harry, looks at me, his forehead wrinkled in confusion. "A bird called Harry Brambling?"

"It doesn't have the Harry part . . ."

He laughs, drowning me out. He's got a really deep laugh. It sounds too big for his thin body. For a second it feels like he's making fun of me, like the boys at school do when I say I go bird-watching on the weekend with Dad.

"I'd love to migrate to Norway," he murmurs.

I get up quickly. The tears want to come again. I can feel the lump rising in my throat.

"Hey, I didn't mean . . . ," Harry starts to say.

I shake my head to make him quiet. "I've got to go back." I look around to find where I came from.

Harry points at an exit. "Third Floor, C Wing. Ward down the corridor from mine."

I stare at him. "What is?"

"Coronary Care, where all the heart stuff happens. Is that where you're going?"

I shake my head. "Not yet. We're just waiting in the Emergency Room."

His face falls a little and again he glances at the bag of liquid. "I know all about waiting," he murmurs. Then he jerks his head toward the entrance I've come from. "Back there, then," he says. "The ER."

He leans back in his seat, looks out at the café customers. I almost ask him what he's waiting for, or who. But I still don't trust my voice. I take a step away. It feels as though I've been gone for ages. What if something's happened to Dad? I take a final look at Harry. I don't know him, I'm sure of it. He's just friendly. Or trying to be, anyway.

He stands up, too. He's careful not to jolt the tube going up his arm as he does. "I'll look out for you . . ."

He raises his eyebrows, waits again for me to tell him my name.

"Isla," I say quickly, then explain it the way I always have to. "Like an 'I' and a 'la,' but spelled with an 's' in between."

Harry nods. "Like an island."

"I suppose."

I think he's about to say something else, but I turn away from him. I feel stupid for talking about bramblings. I feel stupid that he almost saw me cry.

He moves aside as I pass. "Look after your dad," he says softly.

Mum and Jack are waiting for me when I get back to the room, and I feel guilty immediately for being gone so long.

"What's happened?" I ask.

"They've stabilized him," Mum says. "They're moving him up to Coronary Care."

"We're going home with Granddad," Jack says. His face is set as he looks at me. "Mum's staying here until there's more news, then she'll call us when we're allowed to come in. We'll probably have to stay there all night."

I look at Mum. "But I don't want to."

"Neither does Jack, honey. But it's that or wait in here all night. They'll only let me in to see Dad right now, and they might not even do that."

"But I was with Dad when it happened. They should let me see him!"

I hear my voice squeak up at the end. I know I sound like a little kid, but for that moment I don't care. I just want to be near Dad. Jack sighs loudly.

"I'm waiting outside," he says.

I watch him walk through the waiting room. He slips between the sliding glass doors and heads toward the parking lot. Mum takes my shoulders.

"It's just for tonight," she says softly. "Maybe only a few hours, just until they know Dad's OK again." She gives me this thin smile and I know she's telling the truth. "I'll tell Dad you love him," she adds. Her bottom lip is quivering slightly as if she's on the verge of tears.

I'm about to turn and follow Jack out the door when she calls me back. "You'll be OK with Granddad?" she asks softly. "You don't mind?"

I shake my head quickly. But I do mind, really. I don't think I've ever spent a night at Granddad's before. And I don't have any stuff with me. I want to ask Mum why Jack can't just look after us at home. But I don't. Jack's probably already asked, and Mum looks like she's about to crack as it is. I don't want to make it any worse.

"I'll call as soon as I know anything," she says.

I go outside to find Jack. He hasn't gone far. I spot him sitting on the curb, near where the ambulances come in . . . near where Dad came in.

"Don't think I'm happy about it, either," he mutters.

He has a handful of small stones in his hand and he's flicking them at the ambulance tires. I want to sit right up close to him for warmth, but he'll only shrug me off now. We wait for about five minutes before Granddad pulls up in his old brown station wagon. He creaks open the driver's door, gets out to find us. He looks flustered and old, out of place amidst the bright flashing lights. He squints as he peers into the ER waiting room. Then he sees us on the curb and shuffles over.

We look up at him. None of us says anything. Again, Granddad's eyes go back to the waiting room and I think he wants to ask something about Dad. But he doesn't. Maybe he doesn't know what to say.

"Dad's had an arrhythmia," Jack explains, saying the word slowly, like he's trying to remember it.

I can tell by the way Granddad flinches that he knows what this is, which is more than I do. But I guess it must be the heart attack thing that happened when Dad was in the field.

Jack chucks another stone at a tire. Hits a hubcap. For a second Granddad looks as if he's going to tell him off, then stops himself. "We'd better get going, then," he says, twisting his hands over each other.

"Don't you want to see Mum?" Jack stops chucking the stones.

Granddad nods back at his car. "I can't park there," he

says. An ambulance starts up, making him jump. "And she's got enough on her plate."

He nods quickly, several times, which only makes him look more flustered. Then he turns back toward his car, and we follow. He opens the doors for us and Jack takes the backseat, flopping down right across it. So I get in the front.

"Put your seat belt on," Granddad says as he closes his door.

When he pulls out from the hospital parking lot, everything gets even darker. The roads are pretty empty. I look out at the fields. Have we passed the one where Dad fell down? I can't be sure.

Granddad doesn't say anything, which is good. I don't feel like talking. The wave is still in my throat, ready to gush out into tears at any moment. Maybe Granddad's thinking about the last time we were all in the hospital together, when Nan died. He was the one who stayed there then, not Mum. I sat with Dad on our couch as he waited by the phone.

When we get back to his house, Granddad goes straight to the kitchen. With his head in the cupboards, looking for something to eat, he asks me about Dad. I tell him how we were running to the swans when it happened.

Granddad glances at me. Something flickers over his face, an emotion I can't quite read.

"The swans again," he murmurs. I don't know why.

He opens the fridge and starts rooting around. He pulls out some frozen fish fillets from the small freezer section. "These do?"

Jack rolls his eyes, then slopes off to pet Dig.

I fold my arms. "That all you got?"

"I'm afraid so."

We find some pretty soft broccoli and several large potatoes that look like they've been sitting under the sink for years. But there's vanilla ice cream, too. I help him chop the potatoes into thick strips, cutting around the green and knobbly parts, and put them in the fryer. Granddad's hands shake as he places the broccoli into a pot of boiling water.

We eat sitting on the couch, with the news on. There are car bombings and floods and a kid who has been abducted. I just feel numb, watching it all. I don't care about all these bad things happening to other people. I just care about Dad, about the bad things happening to us. Jack pushes his fish to the side of his plate and hides bits of broccoli underneath it. I don't eat much of mine, either. Only Granddad manages his whole fish; he stares straight ahead at the TV and shovels it in. Maybe, being a vet, illness and emergencies are pretty normal, but it feels like he's not even upset about Dad.

Mum calls when we're eating the ice cream. She speaks to Jack first, but I get close to the receiver and listen. I hear her thin, high voice telling Jack that Dad's still stable but that she hasn't been in to see him yet. She says that we might be able to visit in the morning. She's staying there overnight.

"Why can't I take the bus back and wait with you?" Jack says. "Anything's better than waiting here."

Granddad looks up from his armchair then, and Jack shuts up. When I speak to Mum, she sounds so tired. I keep asking her again and again how Dad is. It's horrible being here in Granddad's quiet house when Dad's just down the road, needing us. As I'm talking to Mum, my ice cream pools into milk. I don't feel like eating it after that. When I hang up, I let Dig lick the bowl.

Granddad pulls out some sleeping bags from a closet and asks us where we want to sleep. "There's the spare room, or the couch," he says. "Or you could stay in the cottage."

I remember the last time I was in that cottage, in the clinic part with Dad and Granddad and the dying swan. I wonder if it died there, wonder where it is now. I shudder suddenly.

"I've got the spare room," I say.

Jack glares daggers. "Fine. I'll take the cottage. I'll sleep on the operating table."

But I know he won't really sleep in there by himself. Not with all those animal ghosts. He'll end up on the couch after Granddad goes to bed.

When the TV switches to some show about air disasters, I decide to go to bed early. I take the stairs up to the spare room and lay the sleeping bag on the bare mattress, putting my glass of water on the bedside table. There's a layer of dust, thick as moss, and the room smells of old clothes and emptiness.

Granddad's house isn't like where we live in the middle of town. Here, I can't hear passing traffic, or people out on the street, or police sirens. I lie really still, but there's only the wind moving the tree branches about. I can't even hear the murmur of the television anymore. Maybe Granddad and Jack have gone to bed already, too.

I watch the moonlight making patterns on the carpet. It doesn't make me sleepy. I just keep thinking of the swans in that field and Dad falling down, just keep worrying about what I could have done differently.

So I do what I always do when I can't sleep. I shut my eyes and imagine that I'm really young. Then I imagine Dad is beside me with the fat book of Hans Christian Andersen tales on his lap. He knows the one I want, even before I say. *"The Wild Swans."* I imagine lying back against the pillow as Dad reads the words I know by heart. It's the story of the brothers who are turned into swans. Only it's not a good thing; it's a punishment. Their sister has to rescue them by knitting magic shirts for them to wear. The pictures are beautiful, all pastel-shaded and dreamy-looking; the swans have silver- and gold-edged wings. Dad always lowered his voice when he read the part about the sister weaving stinging nettles into the shirts. He always looked a little disappointed at the end, though, almost as if he didn't want the swan-brothers to turn back into humans again.

I roll over, thump the musty-smelling pillow. I wonder if Dad's awake now, if he feels any better. I clasp my hands together and silently hope that nothing happens in the night. I take my phone from my bag and place it on my pillow, just in case Mum calls. I turn up the ring volume.

Still, I don't want to sleep. I shut my eyes and wait. I stretch my arm out across the pillow so that it brushes the phone; this way I'll feel it if it goes off. For some reason, I remember Harry and the bag of fluid attached to him and the tubes going up his arm. I imagine there's a bag attached to me, too. Only it's not saline seeping into me, but sleep, turning me heavy.

I dream of swans. There are hundreds of them, circling above me.

I stand below them and count. One, two, three . . . But as soon as I give the birds numbers, they stop beating their wings. They drop from the sky. Twist and tumble into the field below. I try to stop counting. Try to shut my mouth. But I can't. I keep saying the numbers.

The birds keep falling.

I'm killing them. I know I am. It's my fault they're all dying. But I can't stop.

I'm really hot when I wake up. The sleeping bag is all tangled around my legs. I lie back and look at the ceiling, try to get rid of the images of the swans falling from the sky. For a second I don't know where I am. Then I remember.

Dad's sick.

I'm at Granddad's.

I look at the phone on the pillow. There's a message from Mum, probably why I woke up. Suddenly, I feel sick. My hands are shaking as I pick up the phone.

> Call me when you get up, sweetheart.
> Dad's a bit better. Love Mum xxx

I breathe out slowly. Check the time. 7:30 a.m. This time last week I was getting up to watch the swans with Dad. It feels like a lifetime ago.

I get dressed in yesterday's muddy clothes. Comb my fingers through my hair, which is still tangled with bits of grass and dirt. I pad downstairs and shake Jack awake. His eyes blink to focus on me and then widen when he remembers about Dad, too. I nod at him.

"Yeah," I say. "You didn't dream it."

Granddad's already in the kitchen, making coffee in a small silver pot on the stove.

"Your mother called," he says. "I'll drop you off there soon."

Dig's trying to sit on Granddad's feet, getting in the way. Granddad hands me a cup. It smells so strong. I never have coffee at home, only hot chocolate or maybe tea.

"Sugar, yes?" Granddad pushes across the sugar container. The sugar has stuck together in clumps, but I manage to get a spoonful. I hover there, unsure whether I should be saying something. I want to know if Granddad is worried about Dad; if this is like what happened with Nan all those years ago. But I just stir the sugar into my cup and stare out the window at the fields behind Granddad's house. I can see the dip in the land where the field turns into Granddad's lake.

I squint as I see something, then sort of choke on what I'm swallowing. There are birds there. They're swan-shaped. Whoopers? Without even thinking about it, I glance around the kitchen for a pair of binoculars. Of course there aren't any; Granddad hasn't been interested in birds for years.

But he does come over to the window and stand beside me, looking out at where I'm staring.

"They're just geese," he says.

I look carefully, waiting for the light to glint onto their feathers and show me that they're white. But it doesn't and Granddad's right. The birds are geese, not swans. Canadas, probably.

"Scavenger birds," Granddad mutters. "Farmers shouldn't sow winter crops if they're not going to protect them."

He shakes his head quickly, his fingers tightening around his coffee cup. I'm surprised by the anger in his voice. He used to like birds, whatever kind they were. The first bird I ever remember watching was when I was with Granddad. It was only a robin, but Granddad made it seem so special. He stopped us mid-footstep and made us stand so quiet, finger to his lips. The robin turned its head and looked right at me. I didn't breathe out until it flew away.

Today, Granddad's not interested in watching geese. He goes into the living room, stops beside Jack to shake him awake again. But Jack's not asleep, he's just lying there. I go in and sit next to him, give him the coffee Granddad's made me. He takes it without a word. He's got a crease mark from the couch down the side of his face.

"It's hot," I say.

He gulps it down without tasting it. It doesn't look like he's slept a wink.

*G*randdad drives us to the hospital. I watch the fields all the way, hoping for a glimpse . . . something to tell Dad. There are no swans. The sky is gray and empty of all birds except gulls. Granddad keeps his eyes fixed on the road in front.

He doesn't park the car, just hovers near the entrance.

"Aren't you coming in?" I ask.

Granddad shakes his head. "I don't like hospitals, remember?"

Jack slams the back door. Granddad and I watch him stomp to the entrance. I unclick my seat belt slowly, then pause with my hand on the door handle.

"Do you want me to give Dad a message from you?"

"Yes, if you want." But he doesn't say what.

Granddad squints as the sunlight comes in through the windshield. I'm angry with him for a moment, like Jack is.

He can't hate hospitals forever just because Nan died in one.

"I'll see you next time, then," I murmur.

I run to catch up with Jack. We don't go through the ER waiting room, and I'm glad about that. Instead we go through to the huge entrance hall that I found last time. It feels different today, not as busy. I look at the line of blue plastic seats near the fake palm trees, checking for Harry. Today there are two elderly ladies sitting there and a man with a walker. But no boys with IV stands and chestnut eyes. I scan the rest of the chairs. Maybe I just imagined him.

Jack's waiting in a corridor under a sign that says *To All Departments*. He's got his arms crossed. "If you're any slower, Dad will have died by the time you get there," he says. Then he looks away, immediately guilty.

He turns, dashes into an elevator. He holds the doors for me. I glance at the list of hospital departments on a board outside: *Urology; Oncology; Phlebotomy*.

"How do you know where to go?" I ask.

"Mum told me."

We get out at Floor Three, and Jack leads me down more wide, shiny corridors. There are signs leading off each side, pointing to departments with more long words. I have no idea what they all mean.

Jack hesitates in front of closed double doors. The wall beside it has a sign saying *Coronary Care Unit*. I remember Harry again, how he told me about this place.

Mum comes bursting through the doors. She hugs us to her, then leads us into the ward. She pauses by a big desk in the circular entrance space. Directly off it are three rooms with beds in them, and there are nurses everywhere.

"I'm only allowed to take one of you at a time," she says, looking from me to Jack. "Dad's still quite sick."

"I'm first," I say. "I have to be." I was the one who was with Dad when it happened, after all.

Jack folds down one of the plastic seats attached to the wall and stares straight ahead at the desk.

"Don't be long," he mutters. "I want to see him, too."

Mum takes my hand. "You ready?"

We walk into a long thin room. There are blue curtains on each side, hanging from the ceiling and wrapped around some of the beds. There are machines everywhere, things beeping and whirring. But it's still quieter in here than the rest of the hospital. Mum stops at the last bed on the right-hand side. She pulls back the curtains slowly and silently.

"Graham? I've brought Isla," she says.

I crane around her to see. And there's Dad, with his eyes shut and his head on the pillow and with tubes coming out of his nose. Wires lead out from under his sheets, too, and plug into some sort of monitor. I don't know what I was expecting, but it wasn't this.

"Is he OK?" I ask. "He still looks sick."

Mum nods. "He's fallen asleep; he was awake just before."

She puts an arm around my shoulders and hugs me to her. She smells of coffee and stale clothes. She must be tired, after being here all night.

"Where did you sleep?" I ask.

Mum nods at the stiff-looking chair beside the bed. "Believe me, you had the better deal at Granddad's."

She tries to smile. Her eyes are like slits. I lean down and touch Dad's hand. His skin is warm and dry, not damp and cool like it was yesterday.

"What happens now?" I ask Mum. "Is he coming home?"

Mum shakes her head. "The doctors want to monitor him. What happened yesterday . . . it was pretty serious. His heart stopped beating regularly, went into a different rhythm entirely. They need to fix that before they can let him go home."

"He'll be OK, though?" I ask, my eyes fixed on his chest, which is rising slightly, then falling. "I mean, he won't . . ."

My words crack and fade. Mum grasps my shoulders tighter.

"We'll know more in a few days," she whispers. "Don't worry, he's not going anywhere."

I want to believe her, but Dad looks so sick. His eyelids flutter as he starts to wake up. I lean toward him. Dad smiles slightly as he focuses. He looks from me to Mum and back to me again.

"Sorry I gave you a scare, Bird," he whispers. His voice is soft as a dandelion head.

I lean closer. "You almost better?"

"Getting there." Again, there's a wisp of a smile on his lips. "Did you find the swans?"

"Don't worry about that now," I say hoarsely.

He tries to say more then, tries to talk about what happened. But his words float away before he finishes full sentences. It's not long before Mum squeezes my shoulders again.

"Let's bring Jack in before Dad's too tired," she says softly. "I'll meet you in the café in twenty minutes or so?"

I touch Dad's hand again. I don't want to leave him. I'm scared that the moment I do, something will happen. I hesitate with my hand on the curtain, not wanting to take my eyes off him.

"I'll be OK," he murmurs. "Promise you won't worry?"

But how can I promise that when it feels like it's all my fault? If I hadn't agreed to go looking for the swans, this might never have happened.

Mum gently presses my back. "It's all right, Isla. Go on and get Jack," she says again. "Dad's in the best place."

But each step I take away from Dad feels wrong. It's as if my feet are made of magnets and they're pulling me back to him.

Jack stands when he sees me. His chair flips back with a thud.

"How is he?" he asks.

I stare at him blankly, my hands still feeling like they're grasping the curtain. "He's kind of quiet."

"But better?"

"I hope so."

I walk away in a daze. Push open the doors to the rest of the hospital and just stand in the corridor. I can feel the wave in my throat again, trying to gush out. I want to curl up in a ball right there in the middle of the corridor and cry. But there are people everywhere and there's nowhere to hide. I concentrate on placing one foot in front of the other. I don't know where I'm going, and I don't want to walk even farther away from Dad, but I know Mum's right. Dad's in the best place. All those machines and tubes have to be helping somehow.

I walk until I can feel the wave sinking down a little. I brush my hand against the walls and look into the rooms I'm passing. Most of them are just waiting rooms, or more corridors leading off to somewhere else. But there are a few wards that I can see right into.

I pause beside one of them and look. The people in these beds are sitting up and watching TV . . . a few of them reading. They don't have tubes in their noses, or curtains around the beds. No other patient looks even half as sick as Dad does. None of them come close. I wonder then whether Dad is the sickest person in the hospital.

I turn the corner. The walls in this corridor are light blue. I don't know how I'll find my way to the café, but a part of me likes the walking around. It's getting my head together.

Then I see him. Though I don't recognize him at first because he doesn't have the IV stand. But I can tell by the scruffy reddish hair that it's him. It's Harry. It's weird, but I feel almost relieved he's here. I take a step down the corridor, toward him. He's leaning up against a doorway, looking in. His expression somehow reminds me of what I was just doing in the other doorways: watching the patients to see who's the sickest. As I get closer, I see that he's looking into some sort of waiting room. I hover just behind him, but he hasn't got a clue that I'm here.

"Hey," I say softly, then worry he hasn't heard me because it takes him awhile to turn around.

But he does. He looks almost embarrassed when he sees it's me.

"You keep turning up."

"It's because my dad's in . . ."

"Coronary Care. Of course. Just down the corridor."

I bite my lip, silent, then look back at the waiting room. "What are you doing?"

Harry looks, too. "Dunno, really. Guess I just like watching other people."

I frown, but he doesn't offer me any more. His cheeks are pinker today, and he doesn't look so pale. He's got a sweater on over his pajamas.

"Are you still sick?"

Harry smiles, but his eyes are sadder somehow. "I'm always sick." He pushes himself away from the doorway. "I can show you around if you like?"

He's walking away from me before I have the chance to reply. I hesitate before following him. Does he even want me to? But he glances back at me.

"My ward's next door," he says. He stops beside a closed door a few feet ahead. "Want to see?"

I do, sort of, or at least I don't want to go down to the café yet to hear how sick Dad really is. But this feels weird. I don't even know him. Why is he being so friendly?

"I should go back," I start to say.

Harry shrugs, then turns to press numbers into a keypad beside the door. He waits for it to click, and holds it open.

"It's kind of crazy in here," he says, nodding toward the corridor beyond. "Very different than Coronary Care." He keeps holding the door for me.

So I go through.

The first thing I notice is that everything's pink. Bright pink. The walls and the floor, even the desk at the entrance and the chairs next to it. The only thing that's not is the ceiling, which is a sky blue color with cloud shapes painted on it here and there. There's noise, too. I can hear music and talking and a television show, and a young child is crying. Harry leads me through the center of it all. He waves at a nurse who's walking toward us.

"This is Isla," he says to her.

The nurse raises her eyebrows at me as we pass and I wonder if she thinks I'm Harry's girlfriend. I look away quickly, glance at a clock on the wall: 9:45 a.m. Mum will be at the café soon.

I peer in the rooms leading off the corridor, trying to understand it all. There are children everywhere: in the beds, playing games with parents, sitting on couches in a bright purple room. A small boy with no hair at all walks past us.

"What is this place?" I murmur.

"Children's cancer ward."

That stops me in my tracks, right in the middle of the corridor. "You have cancer?"

Harry turns back to me, his forehead wrinkling a bit. "Well, I'm not in here for fun." He watches me carefully. "Acute lymphoblastic leukemia. Mad, hey?"

He makes a face. But I don't laugh like I think he wants me to. I'm too confused. I try to keep from staring at his hair. It looks so thick. He doesn't look like he has cancer.

"Are you sure?"

He squawks out a laugh. "I think three years of treatment's pretty sure. But right now I'm in remission, which means the cancer's gone away for a while, so they're only topping me up with chemo when I need it." He catches my gaze. "And my hair's hanging in there, just. A few days more, though, it might be a different story."

"But you don't even look sick," I say. "Not today, anyway."

"That's cos I've got someone else's blood in me." His eyes twinkle as they register my confusion. He leans toward me to whisper, "Blood transfusion: I'm not a vampire . . . in case you were wondering."

I smile a little then. He's so confident. He's acting like it's the most natural thing in the world that he has cancer. But he must be pretty sick. Maybe even as sick as Dad. In a room opposite us, there's a girl staring at me from a bed.

She looks exhausted, barely awake. Suddenly, I feel as if I'm intruding.

"Am I even allowed here?" I ask. "It feels kind of weird."

"You're with me, it's fine."

"I don't even know you, not really."

"Does it matter? I don't know any of the other kids in here, either." He starts walking again. "Besides, it's a pediatric ward, so there's no visiting hours."

"A what?"

"Pediatric. It's a ward for 'young people.'" He rolls his eyes. "Yeah, they think we get lonely, so in here it's always open house. Visitors can come whenever. Anyway . . ."

He stops beside an open door. I look into the room. There are two beds, but only one looks like it's been slept in. The walls are lime green and there's a big flat-screen TV opposite the beds and really ugly paintings above them. It looks about as different from Dad's room as possible.

"I'm the oldest one in the ward," Harry explains. "So I don't have to share with anyone, not if I don't want to."

"This is your room?"

"For the moment . . . If someone has to go into isolation, I might have to move."

I think he wants me to go in, but I hesitate. I mean, it's kind of his bedroom, after all. Apart from Jack's, which doesn't count, I've never been in a boy's room. "How long have you been here?"

He thinks. "On and off, for the past three weeks. I was getting treatment at home before that. But Mum kind of needs to go back to work, so they brought me in."

He walks ahead of me into his room. "Come see my view," he says.

His window stretches across the whole of the wall; it's so much bigger than the window in Dad's ward. It lets in loads more light. He walks over to it. The sunshine turns his skin pale as a ghost.

"Don't worry, you can't catch it from me."

I feel my cheeks flush, so I look away from his grin and to the window. I can see a lake, surrounded by trees, and I start forward before I even realize what I'm doing. My eyes scan across the water, checking to see if the whoopers have gone there.

"I've been watching that lake for ages," Harry says. "I almost told you yesterday, when you said about the Harry Bramblings. Think there's any down there?"

I glance over at him to see if he's teasing. But Harry just holds my gaze, genuinely interested.

"Maybe," I say quietly. "It's a bit early for them yet."

His face falls. "So what do these bramblings look like?"

"They're kind of small, orangey . . ."

"Kind of like me, then." He points to his orangey hair.

I can't help but smile. "A little. You'd never see one from up here, though."

I turn back to study the lake. There's a clump of ducks in one corner, and something else darting in and out of the reeds along the edge. We're too far away to see clearly.

Then something bigger comes into focus. I can't tell whether it's a whooper or a mute from here, but it's definitely a swan. Its feathers look grayish and young. There's just the one. My breath catches in my throat as I think about that lone gray whooper flying away from the power cables that day . . . all on her own. Perhaps it's her.

"What is it?" Harry asks.

"Just a swan. Maybe a whooper. Maybe part of the flock we've been chasing."

"Chasing?"

I turn to Harry to explain how Dad and I always watch the whooper flock, how they didn't settle on their normal wintering grounds because of the new power lines. "The flock is what Dad and I were following when he had his heart attack thing," I say.

Harry's mouth turns down at the corners. "I didn't mean to bring up your dad," he says.

"It's OK." I turn back to the window and try harder to work out if it's a whooper. "Dad will cheer up once I tell him there's a swan here. Honest."

"Really?"

"Yeah." I smile. "He's kind of obsessed with them."

*H*arry takes me down to where the café is.

"You'll be OK with your mum, yeah?" he asks in the elevator.

"You can meet her if you like," I say.

"Nah." Harry shakes his head, looking suddenly embarrassed. He gets out of the elevator and points to where I can already see the café in the entrance hall. Mum and Jack are sitting at a table to the side. Mum looks up and sees me. I wave, feeling a little guilty that I'm late.

"See you around," Harry says. "Remember, it's an open access ward, so you can visit whenever."

"I'll try."

Mum pushes a paper cup of hot chocolate toward me. It's lukewarm. "We thought you'd got lost," she says.

"Sorry. I kind of did." I press my face into Mum's neck in a sort of hug.

Jack's frowning when I look at him. "Who was that?" he asks. He looks back to the elevators, to where Harry must have disappeared.

I shrug. "Just a boy I met in the hallways. His name is Harry."

Mum laughs a little, though I think she's more puzzled than happy. "Only you could make friends in a hospital, babe. Can you drink that on the go?"

I nod, trail behind her with the cup in my hand. We're silent in the car. Mum's really tired, and I think Jack must be shocked by how Dad looks.

"What happens next?" I say quietly.

Mum looks at me in the rearview mirror. "They're going to do some tests, see what the problem really is. He might have to have an operation later in the week. But he's stable, for now. You don't need to worry."

But her words don't sound certain enough.

When we get back to the house, Jack gets his soccer ball from the garage. "I'm going to the park," he calls back to Mum.

"Can I come?" I say quickly. I don't want to go in the house yet, don't want to sit with Mum and not know what to say about Dad. I'd rather talk about something else, even if it is with Jack's friends. If Saskia were here, I'd go to her house.

Jack hesitates, scrunches up his face as he thinks. It's obvious he doesn't want me there, but he nods anyway.

Perhaps he feels sorry for me. He kicks his soccer ball down the street, bouncing it off telephone poles and small front walls. I hang back a bit.

There are four of Jack's mates waiting at the playground: Deano, Jez, Rav, and Crowy. I already know them all. They're sprawled on top of the wooden kiddie castle, legs hanging down over the climbing wall. I glance quickly at Crowy, but of course he's not looking at me. He's got his head down, drawing something with a marker onto the top of the slide. His long hair falls down across his face. I force my eyes away before he looks up and finds me staring.

There are a couple of girls from Jack's grade there, too, perched on the swings. Jack glances over at me when he sees them, and I know what that look means. *Don't be a jerk, Isla, don't make me look stupid in front of everyone.* I smile at them all. One of the girls does this little half wave at me. I recognize her from the all-ages sports team from summer. I think her name is Jess. I'm about to ask her when Deano and Jez call down "hi" to me. They're friendlier than usual. Perhaps Jack's already told them about Dad, how I was the one who had to call the ambulance. I look back at Crowy, but I don't think he's even noticed I'm here yet.

I drape myself around the far pole of the swings. It's hard to look like I fit in when I know they all think of me as Jack's little sister. So I just watch Jack smack the ball against the climbing wall. The ball bounces off the fake rocks that are stuck there and comes back to him at awkward angles. Jack lifts his knee and stops it easily. He's so good at controlling the ball, at moving it to the places he wants it to go. So much better than me.

Jess, the girl who half waved, tries talking to me, starts asking about my weekend, and I wonder whether she knows about Dad, too. I tell her, briefly, skim over what happened. She nods politely and puts her features into an expression that looks almost sympathetic. Maybe she's just trying to impress my brother. I don't know. Either way, I feel really awkward talking about this with her. She's making all these soothing noises like she actually cares. When the conversation dries up, I look down at where my sneakers are scuffing into the woodchips. I want to ask her about her weekend, but it feels really stupid now, after what I've just said about mine.

The boys jump down from the castle to play soccer, and there's this awkward moment where I don't know whether to go with them or to keep hanging with the girls. But Crowy stops and looks back at the swings.

"We need to even up our teams," he says. He must be talking to all of us girls, but for a second it feels like he's just talking to me. He flashes a grin then, one of those perfect ones where his teeth seem so white and straight. And then he really does look at me. "You're a good player," he says, raising his eyebrows. "How about a game?"

The other girl on the swing giggles as Crowy jogs away. I hear her mumble something as I start to follow him. I turn around.

"I'm sure you could both play, too," I say. "The boys won't mind."

The girls just smile and shrug. "Maybe later," Jess says.

They're not really dressed for soccer, I can see that now. It's probably the last thing they had in mind.

The boys mark goals with their sweatshirts. I play on Jack and Crowy's team. I'm glad about that, glad Jack's letting me play with him. Glad Crowy is, too. I glance around at the others. No one seems annoyed that I'm here, no one even cares. They just want to get on with the game.

"If you get the ball, just run it down," Jack says to me quietly. "Then pass it back to me. Don't try to shoot."

He knows as well as I do what I'm good at. I breathe out slowly, stretch the muscles in my legs. My body's tingling to run, desperate to stop thinking about Dad.

Jack kicks the ball deep into the other half to start the game. Deano's onto it immediately, but Crowy slides in and steals the ball from him. He's really good, maybe even better than Jack. I keep out of the action for a while, watching the way they exchange passes. They keep pace with each other, running down the field. They seem to always know where the other one's going to be. It reminds me of how the swans fly: that silent communication and support . . . that perfect formation. I watch Crowy sidestep around Deano and then Rav, twisting with the ball, then flicking it across to Jack. He makes it look so effortless.

Jack stops for a moment to push the hair from his eyes. He sees me and hesitates. But I'm in a good position. He holds my gaze as he kicks the ball cross-field toward me. I stop it with a soft thud. Control it. It's my big moment, my chance to prove myself. But already Deano's running toward me. I have to be quick. I head out to one side and really run. It's clear up ahead; everyone else is still back near Jack. I don't think they were expecting him to kick the ball to me. I focus on getting to the makeshift goal, focus on knocking the ball ahead of me. I stretch out my legs. It feels good. It feels so good to be running so fast, to have everyone else behind me. From the corner of my eye, I see Deano trying to catch me. Jack's running hard, too, speeding down the other side of the field. Even he can't catch me. And he's fast, usually faster than me. But not today.

When I get to the goal, there's still no one anywhere near me. I'm too worried I'm going to miss if I kick it. So I just run the ball straight in. I grin as I do. Pump my fist in triumph. I've just scored my first goal in front of my brother's friends. It feels amazing. I look back at them, find Crowy's face. He's grinning, too, holding his hands up above his head and clapping. Then suddenly Deano and Jack have caught up with me. They're panting hard, and both are glaring at me. I can understand why Deano's mad, but Jack? He jogs over to me, pulls his T-shirt up to wipe his face.

"I said *I'd* get the goals," he growls.

He leans over, placing his hands on his knees to catch his breath. But I feel great, as if I could keep running for days. I poke him in the ribs.

"Aren't you glad I did?" I say, smirking at him.

I start laughing. It starts as a small giggle, but then I can't control myself. I have to sit down on the grass, I'm laughing so much. I press my hands to the damp ground and try to hold it in, but that just makes me snort. Jack looks down at me. He's still glaring at first, wanting me to shut up, but then even he starts smiling. He can't help it.

"You're a loon," he mutters.

"But I'm a fast loon!" I'm still laughing so hard I can hardly get the words out.

"All right, I'll give you that." Jack straightens up, then sticks his hand down for me to grab. He pulls me back up to my feet. "Come on, then, loon, the game's not over just because you score one goal."

When I run back to position, I'm bouncing from foot to foot, eager to do it all again. I look across and see Crowy laughing at me. And then I realize. I haven't thought about Dad once since I got here.

*A*ll the way to school, I try to convince Mum to let me stay with her.

"I just want to be with Dad," I say.

The thought of going back to school now, after this weekend, without Saskia and with everything that's happened, just seems unbearable.

Mum relents in the end.

"OK, I'll ask school if you can miss a day." She catches my eye in the rearview mirror. "But don't think you can make a habit of it."

"I don't know why I can't miss school, too," Jack grumbles.

"Exams, that's why." Mum pulls into the teachers' parking lot and keeps the car running. "I won't be long." She jogs into the office.

I glance around at the rest of the parking lot and hope

that none of my teachers arrive while I'm here. Jack walks slowly to the school gates and Crowy comes out to meet him. I swallow quickly and almost wish I'd walked in with Jack. I watch as Crowy chucks his arm around Jack's shoulder and leans in to whisper something to him. I imagine what it might feel like to have his breath on my ear. Then he starts laughing, pushing Jack away. I stare at his hair, which is way past the regulation collar length, and remember the way he grinned at me yesterday. He doesn't look across for me this time.

Mum comes out of the office and gives me two thumbs up. "Piece of cake," she says as she gets into the car. She turns around to me before she drives off. "The lady said you can have as much time off as you need."

I clamber over the gear stick to get into the front seat. I stick my feet up onto the dashboard and watch the buildings shoot past. Even though I know it's going to be hard to visit Dad, it still feels like I'm escaping. Without Saskia there, school's worse than ever. As Mum drives faster, my eyes follow the edges of the clouds. I imagine I'm a bird flying up there, keeping pace with the car. I'm looking for the whoopers, really, trying to catch a glimpse of them so I can tell Dad.

ad looks a little better than yesterday. Somehow his skin is less gray. But he still looks so weak, as if he's a hundred years older than he was. I stand behind Mum. I don't know how loudly I should talk to Dad; maybe I shouldn't talk at all. It feels like then he might fade away completely. But I want to tell him about how I played soccer yesterday. Dad used to be an amazing soccer player, even better than Jack. I jiggle my legs as I remember how I raced down the field and ran the ball into the goal. Then I imagine that Crowy's there, watching me, and I'm lining up another goal, bringing my leg back to shoot, aiming and . . .

"Ow!"

I blink. Mum's rubbing her shin. I've kicked her leg by mistake.

"What'd you do that for?" she asks, glaring at me.

I look across at Dad, who's staring at me, too.

"I scored a goal yesterday," I blurt out. "When Jack let me play."

Dad looks so pleased then that his eyes almost seem to become brighter for a moment. I'm glad I told him. But Mum folds her arms across her chest.

"Did you have to score it again on my leg?" she mutters.

I lean down and rub her shin. "Sorry, got carried away."

But Mum doesn't really mind. She pushes me to the head of Dad's bed so that I can talk to him more. I notice the way Dad's starting to smile. He's more with it today. He can finish sentences. Perhaps he is getting better after all. Perhaps they'll just do these tests, then let him out in a day or two. I lean up closer to him, ready to tell him the news that I know will really make him smile.

"You were right when you said there was a lake behind the hospital," I say. "And there's a swan on it, too, maybe a whooper."

Dad's eyes really light up then, just as I'd imagined. "Why didn't you say?"

"Only saw it yesterday."

"Is the rest of the flock there?"

I shake my head. "Just one."

I walk over to the window. It's near Dad's bed, but it's probably too high up for him to see out of. I look out for him instead. I only see the parking lot and the roadway and, beyond that, fields.

"Your window's facing the wrong way," I tell him. "You need to go to one on the other side to see the swan."

I glance at Mum but she's shaking her head. "No chance, babe. Dad's got to stay here."

"Can't we even take him in a wheelchair? Just for a look."

"Nope. He's too ill."

I come back to Dad. His smile has fallen a little now.

"You'll have to look for me," he says in his thin, raspy voice. "Keep a watch for the others, too."

I glance across at Mum, but she just rolls her eyes as if to say "you know what he's like." She reaches forward to grab Dad's hand.

"If it will keep your spirits up," she murmurs, obviously just trying to please him. But I swear Dad's cheeks are pinker now that he's interested in something.

And then, suddenly, I know what I'm going to do. I know exactly what I can do to keep Dad's spirits up. I'll go find that swan.

"Can I meet you in the café in an hour?" I ask Mum.

I stick to the edge, following the fence around the parking lot. I can't find an entrance, but there is a shed that seems to sag at the corners, and there is a slit in the fence in front of it. It runs vertically from about shoulder height to the ground. I pull on the wire, testing it. It bends back easily, as if it's been bent like this before. I curl it toward me like a wave, opening up the slit. Then I kick at it, pushing it back farther. I ignore the sign: *Keep Out. Authorized Personnel Only.* Take a breath. Then bend my body through.

I take a few steps. It doesn't look the same down here as it did through Harry's window. There are plastic bags half submerged in the mud around my feet, crushed beer cans and hundreds of cigarette butts. I step across a faded laundry detergent box. I almost turn back. It's obvious I'm not supposed to be here. I don't know what the "Authorized Personnel" would do if they found me. I'm not the first person to have done this, though. I can tell that by the way the ground has been trampled into a path that leads to a patch of trees.

The memory of Dad's face keeps me going. He looked different when I mentioned the swan, excited almost. I try to convince myself that I'm doing the right thing. I step across the manky brown carpet of dead leaves, going deeper into the trees. It gets darker the farther in I go. Everything's so silent. There are no machines whirring on and off, no gurneys trundling past, no patients crying out. I can only hear the wind whispering leaves and bits of rubbish about. It smells better than in the hospital, too, like damp leaves and mud. I wish I could bottle it and take it back for Dad.

I step over another crushed beer can and look ahead to where it's getting lighter. There's a gap beyond the trees. If Dad were here with me he'd walk on confidently, blabbing about how alive it makes a person feel to be out in nature. He'd be stopping to look at beetles in the leaf litter, and touching the trees. He wouldn't be scared at all. There's a real ache in my chest as I think about it. I want Dad here with me. It's not fair that he isn't. I touch the phone in my pocket. I'll just go as far as the lake, take a photo of the swan, have a good look around for any others, and then head back. I won't hang about.

I hear a crack to my left and freeze. The bushes shake. A dark patch of brambles rustles abruptly. Then the movement stops. I stare at the leaves, waiting. A drop of frosty water lands on my head and slides down my cheek. Then something small and black darts out of the bushes. I trip backward over a tree root and almost fall. But it's only a bird. A small coot that's probably as frightened as me.

I get to the lake. The swan is still there. She's not far away, floating on her own. She's smaller and more gray than most, but she's definitely a whooper. Her beak is long and yellow, like all whoopers', but has traces of pink. I don't think she's even a year old. It's weird, but there's something almost familiar about her. I'm sure she's the same bird we saw at the preserve that day, looping above us. I'm sure I've found her. That's already enough to tell Dad. But still, I look across the water and at the banks of the lake.

I go to the edge of the water, toward her. She doesn't move but she seems to be watching me, her small black eyes fixed on mine. She's a beautiful swan, with clean feathers and a long, straight neck. I take my phone out of my pocket and take a photo. She doesn't bob her head away. She doesn't look scared of me at all.

I crouch down and keep watching. Near my feet are some of her chest feathers, a babyish dark gray color. They're soft and damp, a little like fur. I take the two longest ones and run my forefinger and thumb over them, making them smooth and perfect. I put them in my pocket with my phone. I take them for Dad.

When I look up again, she's there. I mean *right* there, in-front-of-my-face there. Close enough to touch. I don't know how she's swum up to me so quickly, or how I didn't notice. Her eyes are still locked on my face. Birds aren't supposed to have expressions, but this swan seems to. She seems curious. It's almost human the way she's looking at me, like she's asked me a question and now she's waiting for my response. I glance away and then back at her, just to check I'm not imagining it. But she's still looking at me like that.

I start shuffling backward up the bank. I move slowly and steadily so she doesn't get alarmed. Even though I'm not scared of swans, I know they're pretty powerful. I mean, everyone's heard stories about swans breaking people's arms with their wings. Granddad told me once that a swan can drown a dog.

"Why are you so brave?" I murmur to her.

She tilts her head as if she's listening. She comes closer. Her feet squelch in the mud as she steps onto the bank. She stretches her wings out and for a moment she's absolutely massive, towering above me. Her wings block the light. I scrabble to stand. She beats her wings, and a stench of stale water hits my nostrils. Already her beak is stretching toward me and her wings are against my shins.

"Shoo!" I say. "I don't have any food."

I turn quickly and jog away from her. I'm not frightened exactly, but there's something odd about this bird.

Wild swans should be timid, scared of humans. This one's different.

I think I'll stop after a few strides, but I don't. I increase my pace. It feels good to run: just like yesterday, playing soccer with Jack, and like last summer, all the practice runs we did on the track team. I glance back to see the swan returning to the water. She's fine now, no longer hungry or whatever it was that made her come up to me like that. I watch her swim away. Maybe she's lonely being here without her flock.

I run instead of thinking too hard about it. My breathing starts to get heavier, and I feel my shoulders drop as I ease into the pace. Then I hear short, sharp smacks on the water, and I turn my head.

It's the swan. She's beating her wings, running on the surface of the lake. At first I think she's following me. Then I realize. She's trying to take off. Trying to get the speed she needs from running across the water. I keep moving. I think she's going to lift off at any moment. But she doesn't. She keeps running across the surface. As she starts to catch up with me, I feel the sweep of wind coming from her feathers. It's almost as though she's racing me.

Then I see her eyes. She's still watching me. I stumble, look across at the trees. There's no one else here. Only me. I stare back at her. I even start to run a little toward her. I'm gasping for breath, sucking the cold wind down into my lungs. Her feet smack harder on the surface of the lake and she inches ahead. It's almost as if she's urging me to go faster as well. It's ridiculous. Swans don't race each other like this, and they definitely don't race humans.

I hear the breath rasping in my throat, the strain in my ribs. I slow down, I have to. The swan watches me, falters for a moment. I wave my arms at her, try to scare her into taking off. Instead, spray splashes from her feet as she lowers her body back to the water and refolds her wings. Instantly she's calm, as if she were never running in the first place.

I collapse onto my hands and knees, and gasp for air. My body's hot, my shirt's stuck to my back. I turn my head sideways to the lake. I take a breath, as long as I can make it, then another. I see her, now floating farther away. Why did she follow me like that? Why didn't she just fly? If Dad were here, he'd probably be able to explain it. Perhaps racing humans around a lake is some strange swan behavior thing that I've never heard of. I don't know.

I wait until the breath stops rattling in my throat before I sit up straight. I watch the swan float farther away. She's so uninterested now. I stand up shakily. I glance back at the track. My footprints are there, dug into the muddy surface. I know I didn't imagine what just happened.

I walk straight through the hospital, taking the stairs two at a time. All the while, I'm starting to doubt it. That swan can't really have been following me. Swans just aren't that interested in humans. Maybe I've gone mad. Maybe it's because I'm stressed. I remember some TV show Mum used to watch, where they talked about how stress affected behavior. The people who were interviewed did all sorts of strange things. Some of them had even hallucinated whole conversations with imaginary people. Perhaps that's what I've done: I've imagined the swan looking at me like that, following me. But it felt so real.

I need to talk to Dad.

Visiting hours are over, but I go to Dad's ward anyway. The nurse at the entrance desk takes one look at me and shakes her head.

"You've got mud on your shoes," she says with a thick

Scottish accent. It's difficult to understand what she means at first.

I look down. All the way behind me there's a trail of marks on the shiny floor.

"But I need to tell him something," I say, my thoughts still full of the swan. "It's important."

I keep the feathers grasped tight in my pocket. If the nurse is unhappy about the mud, she probably won't like them much, either. She pinches her face into that sympathetic look I've seen a lot lately.

"I'm sorry, hen, but you need to have your mum here with you. We can't let you in without her permission . . . even if it were visiting hours."

She comes around the desk and stands close to me.

"Tell you what," she says softly. "Why don't we look in on your dad, together, from the doorway?"

Her voice goes up in pitch, making it sound as if she's talking to a five-year-old. It's not what I want, watching Dad from the doorway with a nurse's hand on my arm. I want to go right up to him and give him the feathers. I want to hug him and ask him about the swan. But what else can I do?

The nurse leads me to the entrance of the ward. She stands behind me, her hands on my shoulders. I feel like a suspect in a cop show; it's as if she's about to march me off to the police station. The curtains are open around Dad's bed, but I can't see him clearly, not from here, not even when I stand on tiptoes. I think he's asleep. He's very still. So still it doesn't look like he's breathing. I feel my heartbeat speed up as I think it. I'm being paranoid. There'd be beeping and alarms and nurses running to him if he stopped breathing. I take a step away. I don't want to imagine it.

"See, hen, he's fine," the nurse coos. "No problems at all. Now what did you want to tell him?"

I shake her off and head for the door. She's calling something else out to me, something about trying to find my mum, but I deliberately block it out. I hate this; I hate all these other people being responsible for Dad . . . controlling when I can see him and what I can say to him. I know it's not how he'd want it.

The door to Coronary Care thuds shut behind me. Already I'm walking down the corridor, and I know where I'm going. I'm going to see Harry. At least he'll be glad to see me. Besides, with the window in his room, he's the only other person who might have seen what happened at the lake.

My shoes make little squelchy noises as I hurry down the corridor. At the door to the children's cancer ward I hesitate. It's locked shut. I lean up against it and peer through the glass section.

Then the door clicks open and I fall through. There's a nurse at the ward desk, smiling at me, her finger on the door buzzer. I think she's the one I saw last time.

"Here to see Harry?" she asks.

"But is he . . . am I allowed?"

She nods. "If it's all right with Harry, it's all right with me."

She leads me down the corridor. It doesn't feel as busy in here today. There's less noise, and fewer people. Not so many visitors. Harry's door is shut. The nurse knocks it gently, opens it an inch, and looks in.

"Isla's here," she says. "You up for it?"

I hang back. I can't hear him reply. What if Harry is

really sick this time? What if he doesn't want to see me? I feel my stomach tighten as I wait. The nurse turns back to me. Gives me a wink.

"Don't stay too long, pet."

She holds the door open for me to go through.

Harry's in bed, propped upright with pillows. He grins when he sees me, beckons me in, but I could be looking at a different boy than the one I remember. Today, there are dark, dark circles around his eyes, and his skin is even whiter. There are a few strands of hair on his pillows. He reminds me of some sort of furry creature, something that would live underground. I half expect him to scurry away, burrow back under the covers.

"Take a seat," he says. "I didn't think you'd come back so soon." There's a questioning look in his eyes.

"Do you want me to go?"

"No way." He shakes his head as if I've said the most ridiculous thing. "You just missed my mum, actually, could have been quite a party."

I move to the chair beside his bed. He looks exhausted, as though he's run a marathon. Suddenly, what happened at the lake doesn't seem so important. Not when Harry looks as sick as this.

"What happened to you?" I ask.

"It's just the chemo. My body doesn't like it too much."

I find it hard to believe chemotherapy could make that

much difference to someone, and so fast. He was so casual about it before. But I start nodding as if I understand.

"Does it hurt?" I say.

Harry thinks for a moment. "I'm not in pain, like how I guess your dad is. But it's just . . . kinda uncomfortable. Everything aches."

His hand flies to his chest and he presses at something through his pajama top. At first I think it's his heart.

"Are you OK?"

He brushes away my concern. "Just my Hickman line."

Again, I don't understand. I chew on my lip. It's as if he's living in a different world from me, knowing about a whole bunch of different things. I'm suddenly too shy to say anything. Whatever I say now is going to sound all wrong. So I look out the window. The lake looks like a blur of color, and I can't see the swan.

"I was watching you, you know," he says quietly. "Out there on the lake." He turns back to me, his pupils smaller from looking at the light.

I find myself nodding again.

"I was actually kind of hoping you were."

We stare at each other. I should be looking away now, but I can't somehow. It's weird, a little like the pull I felt when I was watching the swan. Harry doesn't look away, either. His eyes are shining, as if there are bonfires burning inside them.

"What was going on down there?" he asks. "When you ran around the lake? Did you have food with you or something?"

"I didn't have food."

"Then why was she following you?"

My face gets hot, even my ears go warm. I can't just blurt out how the swan looked at me so intensely, then ran after me across the water. I'd sound like a head case. So I drag my eyes from his and look down at the floor. I wait for Harry to laugh it off, to say something about me being a crazy bird girl. To say exactly what I'm thinking myself: that all of this is in my imagination. But suddenly he's leaning toward me.

"You were on the path and she was on the water," he says quietly. "Her wings were flapping, but . . ."

"She didn't fly, I know." I look at him carefully, check that he's not just making fun of me. But he's not smiling at all now.

"That's pretty weird, isn't it?" he says. "For a swan to do that?"

"Wild swans should be scared of humans," I say. "She wasn't scared of me at all."

"Was she trying to attack you?"

"I don't think so. Swans aren't like that, and I wasn't threatening her."

I don't tell him how, for a moment, it felt like the swan wanted me to go faster. But I want to. I want someone else to understand that there's something different about her. A thought pops into my head.

"Why don't you come with me?" I say. "To the lake? You can see the swan up close then."

Immediately I wish I hadn't asked. Harry is obviously too sick to leave the hospital. He frowns as he thinks, as if he's trying to find exactly the right words.

"I haven't been outside for ages," he says quietly. He stops and looks down at the bed, suddenly awkward.

"Sorry," I say. "I didn't mean to ask you if you're too sick."

He shakes his head. "I could go, maybe. If I got permission from the nurses." He hesitates, still looking at the bed. "I'm just not sure . . ."

I swallow, thinking. Maybe he just doesn't want to go down there with *me*. But if he could see that swan, just once . . . I touch the feathers in my pocket.

"I don't have to come with you," I say quickly. "You could go with a nurse, or your mum, or . . ."

"I want to," he says softly. "It's just . . . it's not easy if something goes wrong. You know what I mean?"

He's trying to tell me something without actually saying it. But I think I understand. Up here, in his cancer ward, there are nurses and painkillers and Hickman lines. Safe things. Things that he's used to. Down there, at the lake, it's different.

"You think it'll make you sicker, going there?"

He folds his hands in his lap. "I'd just rather watch from the window." His voice sounds shaky and quiet.

It makes me wonder. Maybe he's scared. Maybe he's spent so long in bed feeling tired that he's forgotten what it's like to do normal things like walk to a lake. Suddenly, I don't know what to talk about. I want to show him the photos on my phone and tell him more about the swan, but it seems stupid now.

Harry shifts in his bed. "But you'll go down there again, though, won't you?" he asks.

I glance up at him, surprised.

"I like watching you there." He shrugs, looks away. "I like watching. Anyway . . . I don't have much else to do up here, not until my transplant."

I stare at the smooth skin on his neck. "What do you mean?"

"It's where they kill off all the stuff inside my bones and give me someone else's stuff instead."

"Why?"

"It seems mine's pretty diseased. So they'll stick someone else's bone marrow in me and hope my body accepts it."

"When's that going to happen?"

He runs his fingers through his hair, pulling a few strands out. "Dunno, really, a couple of weeks, a month . . . whenever they find a match for me. It's why I'm in here . . . what I'm waiting for." He looks at me quickly. "And until then, I need something to do. So you running around a lake . . ."

He blushes, and all the paleness in his skin disappears for a moment. It's kind of cute. I smile as I get my head around what I think he's trying to say.

"You want to watch me? You want me to run around the lake like I'm your own private TV show? Should I do a dance for you, too?"

The shocked look in his eyes makes me laugh. "You're as nuts as that swan is," I say.

And suddenly he's laughing, too.

I race down to the café. Mum's got a half-eaten cheese sandwich in front of her.

"Sorry," I say.

She raises an eyebrow. "Who is this Harry, anyway? He must be nice if he keeps me waiting twenty minutes."

She's looking at me carefully, wondering.

"He's got leukemia," I say. "I think he's lonely."

She's happy with that explanation. It makes sense. Harry is lonely. Perhaps it's the only reason he wants to be friends with me.

As we begin the drive home, Mum tells me the latest on Dad.

"The parts that lead into his heart, his valves, aren't working properly," she says. "The specialist wants him to have an operation."

"That sounds serious."

"It's major surgery. They have to replace a part of his heart."

"But that means it will work better, doesn't it?"

"Hopefully." Mum looks both ways as she pulls out of the hospital parking lot. "They want to replace one of his faulty valves with a valve from a pig."

"A pig? Seriously?"

Mum smiles slightly. "It sounds a bit odd, doesn't it? Apparently, some parts of a human heart are really similar to a pig's."

"So Dad's going to be part human, part pig . . . half animal?" I frown as I try to understand it.

Mum looks at me, and her smile widens. "You could look at it like that, I suppose."

I lean back against the headrest and imagine Dad turning into a pig . . . developing trotters instead of hands. "It's a shame it's not a valve from a bird," I say.

Mum nods. "Tell me about it. A bird's heart would suit him just fine. He'd probably even look forward to the operation then!"

I tilt my gaze to the gray sky. I can almost imagine Dad up there, circling beneath the clouds, his arms spread wide like wings . . . Half man, half bird. Mum's right: Dad probably would jump at the chance to be like that.

I watch the fields speeding past the window. Soon they start merging into the factories and junkyards outside town, the soft green ground changing to gray. I look down Granddad's lane as we speed past it.

"Do you think Granddad's worried?" I ask.

"About Dad?"

"Yeah."

"I suppose so, in his way."

I remember how Granddad seemed so hesitant when we stayed at his house, how he didn't really speak to us at all. Then I notice shadows flickering across the fields. I look up. There are swans in the sky. A whole flock. I wind down the window, lean my head out to see better. The cold air hits me at full force.

"Isla!" Mum squeals. "It's freezing!"

"But there are swans up there!"

I watch the way they are spaced out, flying in that V shape. There's enough of them to be whoopers. They're honking and trumpeting, and keeping pace with the car, flying in the same direction.

"You should follow them," I say. "Then we can tell Dad we know where they're roosting."

The birds veer across the fields to the left of us. I scan the land, try to figure out where they're heading.

"They're going back to the farms," Mum says. "We can't

follow them. We'll be late for Jack." She leans over the steering wheel to look up at them and the car wobbles for a second. "They make flying look so easy," she says. "But when you see them on the ground, they look clumsy, too big to fly like that."

"Yeah, they transform. That's why Dad likes them."

Mum laughs suddenly. "The first date your dad ever took me on was to watch those blasted birds. He made me get up really early for it, too. He said it would be 'magical.'"

"It must have worked," I say. "You're still with him."

Mum's smile freezes then, and for a moment I think she's going to cry. She looks quickly in her side mirror and signals to pass. We're both quiet. I watch the swans until they get too far away to see anymore. Their feathers glint when the sunlight hits them, and they do look magical for a moment. I wonder what they see from up there, what they think of all the roads and buildings. Do they notice our red car, traveling beneath them?

I close the window and look through the windshield. It starts raining. I turn on the radio to the talk station I know Mum likes. I listen to the drum of drops on the roof and remember the sound of the swan's feet as she ran around the lake beside me.

The traffic becomes busier as we edge into town, and Mum sighs as we reach a new road-construction site. I shut my eyes against the vivid brake lights of the car in front.

I wonder if the lone swan on the lake is a part of the flock we just saw. Perhaps they're heading back now to pick her up. Perhaps she'll run across the lake, take off with them, and that will be the last I see of her. I breathe out slowly. A small part of me doesn't want that swan to leave.

Dreams come easily that night.

I'm down at the edge of the lake, wearing only my thin nightgown. I'm looking at the gray swan. My eyes are locked with hers and I can't look away.

She comes toward me. Her eyes are unblinking. It's as if she wants something, needs something, almost. If I don't give it to her, she's going to tear it right out of my chest.

I turn, try to run. But I can't. My feet are stuck deep in the mud. The swan gets to the bank. Her wide, webbed feet don't sink into the gooey earth like mine do. She stretches her beak toward me. She pecks my thigh. My skin goes colder immediately and pain spreads out from the muscle. I pull up my nightgown and grasp at my skin, try to stop the throbbing. The skin swells, as if there's a blood blister forming. It's agonizing for a second, then fades to a tingling.

She goes around to my other leg and pecks there, too. I scream. Fall backward. Sink into the mud. She pecks my stomach next, my shoulders. Each time there's a stab of pain. I watch where she pecks. The blood blisters are swelling and my skin is moving . . . opening up. Something is sprouting. Small gray feathers are appearing, pushing through the surface. They're all over me. My skin is becoming covered in a swanlike down.

She hisses. She runs her beak over my arms, pushing them out wide across the ground. There's no point resisting. Her touch sends shivers down my spine. I turn my head, look at her small, dark eyes. I suddenly understand what she's doing. The swan is transforming me. She wants me to be part of her flock.

I can't get out of school for a second day.

"Now that they're monitoring him, Dad's going to be fine," Mum says as she pulls up near the gates. "Don't worry."

But I do. I worry all through math, where I don't understand anything anyway, and all through science, where Miss Giles talks about adaptation. Now that Saskia's not here, I don't even have anyone to hang out with. I just sit by myself. And worry.

Art class is different, though; it always is. Mrs. Diver comes up to me right away and asks about Dad.

"I heard what happened," she says. "If you need some more time with your work, or if you just fancy coming in here during lunch period for some peace and quiet, that's fine by me."

She smiles, and I see it's genuine. She puts her arm around my shoulder and leads me away from where I normally sit to another desk where the new girl, Sophie, is already sitting.

"Thought you two could sit together," Mrs. Diver says.

She's trying to be nice, I can see that, trying to bring the two loner girls together. But I'm not really in the mood for talking. Sophie doesn't look very happy about it, either. She looks down at the desk as she moves her stuff over to make room for me. Neither of us says anything.

Mrs. Diver hands out a pile of light blue sheets of paper. Then she turns to her picture of Leonardo da Vinci and drapes her arm across the top of its frame.

"As you know, your major assignment for this semester," she begins, "is to think about flight. We will be working on capturing and then creating the movement of flying. My friend Leo here was one of the first people to be interested in a practical solution to flight. He studied and sketched the things around him that flew, and he used this knowledge to try to design a contraption, a flying machine, so that humans could fly, too. His artistic skills in observation helped him to understand flight, and that's what we're going to try to do, too."

She pulls out pictures from her desk drawer and gets some of the kids in the front row to hold them up. They are sketched drawings: one of something that looks like a kind of hang glider and another of a huge parachute. There are also studies of birds' wings and bats' wings, and diagrams of how da Vinci tried to attach wings to a human body using belts and wood.

"Your task," Mrs. Diver continues, "is to study something that flies. You'll do sketches first, trying to understand and capture on paper the movement of how your study subject flies. Then you can use what you discover to create your own flying model. You can make a simple model of whatever it is you're studying, or you could challenge yourself to use what you've learned about flight to make a flying machine for humans . . . like something da Vinci did. Your models don't have to be big, and they don't have to fly, but I want you to think about capturing the movement of your study subject: its action. You can use da Vinci's sketches as inspiration."

She hands out copies of the sketches so we can look at them more closely. I skip over the hang glider and parachute, but look carefully at his sketches of birds' wings.

I hear Sophie sigh beside me. I guess art isn't really her thing.

"What are you going to study?" she whispers.

She looks away quickly, her eyes darting over everyone else in the room, then back to me. She's shy, really shy, even more shy than me. Suddenly, I feel sorry for her. I look down at the blue sheet on my desk. *Choose something that flies and study its movement*, it says.

"I could do swans."

I wonder about the swan on the lake, whether she's still there. I could easily study her and sketch her. Maybe I could make a flying machine like da Vinci did, but based on swans' wings. Dad would love to have the drawings and the model afterward.

"How will you find a swan to study?" Sophie's leaning over my shoulder.

"Easy."

I explain that Dad's a bird-watcher and how I know where to find them. I don't tell her about the swan on the lake, though. She goes back to reading the sheet.

Mrs. Diver starts talking about things we could base our studies on: bats, helicopters, butterflies . . . I start sketching the outline of a swan. But I can't quite make it look like the swan on the lake. I draw her with her wings stretched out, as if she's flying. That doesn't look right, either. After a while, I realize that Sophie's staring at me. She's holding her chin up with her hand, just watching me draw.

"You know, back home, the swans are black, not white," she says. She sighs again, quickly, turning back to the sheet in front of her. "Everything's different here, kind of the opposite . . . even the birds."

I can sort of understand what she means. Right now it feels like my life has been turned upside down, too.

I take my sketchbook when we go to the hospital after
school.

"I want to draw that swan on the lake for my school
project," I tell Mum, "then I can tell Dad about it later."

She lets me go. I think she's so worried about Dad right
now that she doesn't even really register what I'm doing.

"Meet you in Dad's ward in an hour?"

She nods.

I jog around the edge of the parking lot. I find the wooden
shed and the hole in the fence. I duck through, walk quickly.
There's a dampness in the air, and the smell of earthy,
straggly winter trees. The days are getting shorter and it's
going to be dark soon. I'll need to be quick.

The swan is still there. She's floating in and out of the
reeds, watching me, exactly as I hoped she would be.
It's almost as if she's been waiting for me. She skims her

beak across the water, then points it skyward, swallowing. I tense as I remember my dream, the feel of her beak piercing my skin.

"What's your story?" I murmur. "Why won't you fly?"

I find a tree stump to sit on, then take the sketchbook from my bag and start drawing. Her feathers are so neat across her body, each one stacked in exactly the right place beside the next. Some of them ruffle with the breeze. I try to sketch the feathers on my page so it looks as though they're ruffling, too. She keeps feeding and drinking, not bothered by me at all. She's normal today, just like all the other swans I've ever seen.

The day fades into dusk. I drop my sketchbook back in my bag and clasp my arms tight around me. Stupidly, I left my coat in the car. I breathe out and my breath hangs in the air like a cobweb. I have to stand and move or risk turning into a human icicle. I jiggle my legs and take a couple of steps.

"Will you follow me this time?" I say.

The swan cocks her head to the side as if listening. I clap my hands suddenly and loudly. A couple of mallards take off immediately; she flinches but doesn't back away. I start walking around the track. As soon as I set off, she does, too. She glides across the water, toward me. I shake my head, laugh at her.

"You're weird," I say. "What about if I do this?"

I break into a slow jog. It feels good to move, and my body begins to thaw. I look across at the swan. She beats her wings against the surface of the lake, lifting herself up. She gets faster. Her feet slap on the water until she catches up with me. She doesn't take off. Instead, she watches me.

"Come on, then," I murmur. "Fly!"

Her head is parallel to the water's surface, her neck moving like a snake. Drops of water spin out to me as she edges past. I don't stop this time. I want to know how fast she will go. I want to know if she will take off.

I look at her wings, outstretched now, beating the surface of the water and creating ripples. They're so strong and strange and intricate. While the part of the wing nearest the body keeps still, it's the outer half that beats downward. They look impossible to copy, impossible to make a model of.

She starts to edge ahead. I lengthen my stride, go faster. This time it's me keeping up with her. She doesn't look it, but she's really quick. It feels as if my feet are whirring beneath me as I try to keep pace. Her eyes lock on mine. I stumble a little. Try to keep straight. Keep running. I'm still looking at her eyes when my feet hit something. My body jerks forward, my legs tangling.

I hit the track, still moving, and slide along. I'm almost at the edge of the lake before I stop. Air wheezes out of me and there's mud on my teeth, reeds near my eyes. I wipe the back of my hand across my face. There's blood, a small smear on my skin . . . a trickle running down my cheek.

The swan is still on the lake. She circles back toward me and approaches the bank. I don't move. Her eyes are like dark pools of deep water, keeping me still. She stands in the shallows and flaps her wings, sending a stench of moldy water to my nostrils. She nudges her large, round body toward me.

My breath comes back in a rush as she gets closer. She looks at me so intensely. It's not the way a normal bird looks at humans, all jerky and quick and scared. She's not nervous of me at all. She moves her beak until it stops a few inches from my nose, and I think she's going to peck me. I'm hardly breathing now. My whole body is still and stiff, waiting to see what she'll do. I just hope Harry is watching this. I need someone else to know it's real.

Her beak touches my cheek. I flinch, expecting it to hurt like in my dream. Instead, a bead of cool water drips from her feathers onto my skin. I feel her breath. She smells like damp feathers and reeds. I stay stiller than a stone.

She moves her beak to my neck, touches there, too. I half expect to feel a feather growing from that spot. I'm waiting for the pain. But instead, I go cold. Really cold. A shiver shoots down my spine. Even my fingers go tingly. I keep looking at her dark eyes. It's as if she wants me to understand something.

"I'm imagining this," I say, louder now, so I can hear it and take it in. "This isn't happening."

She moves her head quickly as she hears me. I frown at her, and for a second I think I see a glimmer of confusion in her eyes. Then she lifts her wings. Without thinking, I cower, raising my arms to protect myself. But the wings don't come crashing down. She holds them there, inches from my face, their ends brushing my hair. I glance over them quickly, checking for damage. There are no jagged bones pushing through and no ruffled feathers. They're perfect. Her head moves into a kind of nod, as if she agrees.

"Your wings don't seem to be the problem," I say quietly, as if she could understand. "So what is?"

She folds them slowly, moving away. She lowers her head in submission. Whatever this swan is, she's not angry at me, and she doesn't want food. I stare after her as she slips into the water. She doesn't look back.

I almost don't notice the rain. It's not until the drops soak into my hair and drip down my neck that I feel it. As I'm jogging back to the trees, I decide something. I'm going to come back here, and soon.

I pause under the branches to shake the water from my hair. Strands of it stick across my face. I roll up my pants to see how grazed my legs are, and roll up my shirt-sleeves, too. Everything stings worse than it looks. I pick out tiny stones from the cuts, then roll my clothes back down over them. I dab at my face until it stops bleeding. Then I dash through the rain.

I go through one of the hospital side entrances and get lucky. There's a cart of freshly laundered hospital sheets. My sneakers squeak and slip on the floor as I hurry toward it. I look around to check no one's watching, then pull a stiff folded sheet from a pile and wipe it quickly over my face. I carry it with me as I go up the stairs. I'm still trying to mop water from my hair as I turn into Dad's corridor.

Harry is waiting in the hallway, leaning against the wall near Dad's ward.

"I was watching," he says. He glances over my muddy clothes. "You can't visit your dad like that." He walks down the corridor, away from Dad's ward, then turns to wait for me. "I'm serious, you can't."

I hesitate. I really want to see Dad, I need to tell him about the swan. But Harry's waiting for me, calling back. "Really, they won't let you in, not the way you look. They're paranoid about infections here."

I look down at the mud on my hands.

"Come on, I'll help you clean up," Harry says. "Then you can go back."

I trail reluctantly. He stops by the entrance to his ward and looks through the glass section. "Quick," he calls. "There's no one at the desk. We can sneak past."

He keys in the numbers on the pad and beckons to me. I jog up to him, and he pushes me ahead through the door. We half run, half walk to his room, Harry's hand firm on my back. It feels wrong to be in here, looking the way I do, but it's kind of exciting. Harry shoves me into his room and shuts the door behind us. Then he flings open the closet and grabs two towels. He chucks one at me, and keeps hold of the other. He opens the door a crack, then goes out with the towel. When he returns, he's smiling.

"No puddles on the floor now," he says. "We're safe. I don't think anyone even noticed us; they're probably off getting dinner for the younger kids."

I stand there, shivering. I rub the towel over my sweater and pants, and squeeze more water from my hair. Harry's room is hot as a sauna and, strangely, it makes me shiver even more. I clench my jaw to stop my teeth chattering. I go over to the window. It's getting darker now, but I think I can still see her there, on the lake. For a second I imagine she might be looking up here, finding me, too. Harry comes over with a white shirt, not too different from the school shirt I'm wearing.

"Put this on," he says, handing it to me.

I stare at him.

"At least it's dry." He turns away from me, hops back into bed, and pulls the covers over his head. "I'm not looking."

"But it's yours."

"Just put it on, will you? Or you won't get to see your dad today." His voice sounds muffled from under the blankets. "Anyway, I told you before, you can't catch what I've got."

That's not what I'm worried about.

I glance back at the small window in his door to check that no one's about to come in. Then I go to a corner of the room. I keep my eyes on Harry's bed to check that he's not peeking, either. As quickly as I can, I peel my wet sweater over my head and unbutton my shirt. I let them fall on the floor. I stick my arms through Harry's shirt. It's deliciously dry, like getting into clean bedsheets. My cold, clumsy fingers fumble with the buttons. It's a bit big for me, but when I tuck it into my pants it doesn't look too bad. It smells of pine needles.

"Thanks," I say.

I pick up my sodden clothes, feeling bad about the puddle they leave behind. Harry pops his head out from under the covers. His eyes skim quickly over his shirt on me and I feel my cheeks reddening a little.

"What do I do with these?" I ask.

"Easy," he says. "Chuck them out the window."

He goes across to it, fiddles with a small latch on the side, and then opens it as wide as it goes, which isn't all that far. I look directly below. There's a dumpster, and around it bare concrete.

"Three points if you get it in," he says.

"I can't throw my school clothes out the window! Not into a dumpster!"

"Well, you're not allowed to have dirty clothes in here." He raises his eyebrows at me, nods toward the glass. "It's either you or the clothes. You choose."

He starts laughing, which makes me laugh. I'm laughing too hard when I throw them, and they land with a smack on the concrete. Harry peers down.

"Maternity Ward will have got a shock," he says with mock seriousness. "They're right underneath us."

I think about all those women giving birth, wonder if any baby's first view of the world was of my wet shirt flying by.

I close the window quickly and Harry locks it again. He hops back into bed.

"Thanks again for the shirt," I say. I'm about to head out of the room to catch Dad when Harry calls me back.

"Aren't you going to tell me what happened out there? I was watching you."

So I do. Or I try to, anyway. It's hard to get the words out so they make sense. Plus I don't want to be too long and miss Dad altogether.

"Do you believe me?" I say when I've finished. "About the swan following me and looking at me like that?"

"Weird things happen all the time," he says quietly. "They've happened to me all my life." He glances at his green wall, with its framed pictures of sailing ships and cherry trees. "I'd rather have your weird thing than my weird thing."

He looks back to the window. It's getting black outside now. I can see our reflections in the glass.

"So what are you going to do next?" he asks.

I sigh. "If Dad had been there, he'd know what to do. There's probably a simple reason for why she was following me."

A thought suddenly hits me. I feel stupid for not asking Harry about this before.

"You watch that swan every day, right?"

"Most days. She's only been there about a week."

"Have you ever seen her take off? Fly?"

He shakes his head.

"And have any other swans ever arrived, any of her flock?"

"Never." Harry pushes the covers down and crosses his legs.

"But she must have flown there in the first place . . . so why isn't she flying now?"

Harry chews his lip. "She's forgotten?"

"That would be like us suddenly forgetting how to walk. Birds don't do that."

"Some might, this one might. Are you sure she hasn't had an accident or something? Are her wings OK?"

"I got a close look at them. They seemed fine. No obvious broken bones."

Harry blinks slowly. His eyelids look heavy, as if he's trying to force them to stay open.

"Maybe she just wanted some company," he says.

"How do you mean?"

"Well, if I were that swan and you came to my lake, I might want that, too." He blinks quickly, and I watch a smile grow on his face. "Maybe she thinks *you* can be her flock. Birds aren't famous for their intelligence, are they?"

I remember the intense look in that swan's eyes. "She's not stupid."

"Maybe she just doesn't want to fly, then." He leans over to get his glass of water on the bedside table. He flinches as he stretches across.

"Maybe. You all right?" I ask.

"I'm fine," he says, but I don't believe him. I remember what the nurse said last time about not staying too long.

"I better go."

Immediately he leans toward me with his eyes wide.

"I'll come back," I say. "Don't worry. I just need to catch Dad."

He nods at that. I feel guilty about going, about leaving him on his own.

"I'll watch her for you," he murmurs. "Promise."

I hurry down the corridor. Mum's waiting outside, her arms crossed over her chest.

"Where have you been? Dad's visiting hours are almost over."

"Sorry, I got caught . . ."

". . . in the rain, it seems." Mum looks me up and down, frowns. "I can't take you in like this, you're a mess. And where's your sweater?"

I look down at my feet. "Left it somewhere."

Mum's mouth tightens. "We'll come back tomorrow, with Jack. You can see him then. Dad's tired today, anyway. Let him sleep."

"But I want to see him now!" I bite down hard on my lip. "I've got things to tell him."

"You had your chance," Mum says quietly. "What have you been doing, anyway?"

She's so mad. She's trying to keep her voice steady because we're in the middle of the hospital corridor and there are people watching. She walks ahead of me, and I jog to keep up.

"I'm sorry, I didn't mean . . ."

She spins around. "Dad was looking forward to seeing you, Isla, and you let him down just because you went to look at a swan!"

"But there's time now . . ."

"We need to pick up Jack from soccer practice."

I shut up. I don't even look at her as we go through the parking lot. Mum's bristling with too much anger to talk to me. She drives too fast, goes through two yellow lights. I fold my hands in my lap and look down at them. My stomach feels heavy, as if weighed down by a stone.

Mum pulls into the parking lot next to the school playing fields. Jack gets in. I don't look out for Crowy behind him, not this time. I just keep my head down. Instead, I think of Dad in the hospital, waiting for me. Every inch of me feels guilty. Every mile we drive away from him feels too far. My heart is stretching like an elastic band, stretching between him and here. Something feels like it's going to snap.

The next evening, I take the drawings I've done of the swan and show Dad. I pull out my cell phone and show him the photographs I took, too. He's not so pale today, and he's sitting up in bed. He doesn't look mad at me, either.

"I'm sorry about yesterday," I mumble.

Dad shuffles between the drawings. "I'd rather you were doing these," he says. "They're beautiful."

I take them back from him, embarrassed. "We're studying flight in art," I say. "I'm going to make a model of a flying machine, like Leonardo da Vinci's, but I'll base mine on swans' wings. We have to sketch them first."

"That's hard. Wings are so complex." He reaches over to grab my hand. "I wish I could help."

I think about all the times he has helped me with my school projects, about all the good grades I got when he did.

"You'd be good at making a flying machine," I say.

He laughs, but it's not his usual big laugh . . . it's soft and sad somehow. "Right now I think I need one."

He sighs heavily and turns toward the window. The sky is white as paper through the pane. I want to say something, something to make him forget about his sick heart. So I tell him, finally, about what happened when I went to see the swan on the lake. I watch his face as I talk.

"She followed me," I whisper. "Around the lake."

He hooks his little finger around mine in a fairy's handshake; at least, that's what we always used to call it.

"I think that swan is just curious," he says gently. "Nothing to worry about."

I want to tell him it was so much more than that, explain about the way she looked at me and how she towered her wings over me, but I see how tired he is and I can't somehow.

Instead I nod and say, "Maybe." Because he could be right. That swan could just be curious, and I could be imagining that there's something different about her. I pull out the feathers I took from the lake and give them to him. He holds them lightly and smoothes them out as if they're precious.

"Beautiful," he murmurs, running the edge of them across the back of his fingers. "Like tiny works of art themselves. You should just hand these in."

He struggles to push himself up a little farther in his bed as he looks at me. "You know, real flying machines would never work," he says. "Not ones based on birds, anyway."

He grins and I see for a moment that he's more like he usually is, more excited about my school project than I am.

"My model doesn't really have to fly," I say, reaching forward to make sure his pillows are comfortable.

He keeps grinning. "Go on, ask me why they wouldn't work!"

"OK, why wouldn't flying machines work?"

He leans in to whisper. "Because people aren't birds, that's why." He grabs my arm. "For one of da Vinci's designs to work, the person operating it would need the same muscle power and coordination that a bird would have. But of course, we don't."

"Because birds are too amazing, right?"

He smiles with me. "Sort of. But they've also got hollow bones and huge hearts and more muscles on their bodies than we could ever imagine." His mouth twitches at the edge as he thinks of something. "You know," he begins, "there's something in Granddad's barn that could be useful for you. He's had it since his days at vet school."

"What is it?"

Dad hesitates. "Maybe you remember it from when you were young; you might not like it." He looks up from the feathers, his mouth stretching into a yawn. "Your nan used to call him Old Swanson. Ask Granddad to show you."

His eyes start to close.

"What's Swanson?" I ask.

But he just murmurs as he's slipping into sleep, "Swans *are* amazing, though. Pretty magical."

I grab his hand again, thinking he's going to rattle off facts about whooper swans for the fifty-billionth time. But he doesn't. His eyes flicker open and he gazes at the sky.

"Some say swans' wings catch souls."

I grasp his hand a little tighter. "What are you talking about?"

He wakes up a little then. "It's a myth," he says. "Some people used to think that if you were dying when a swan was flying overhead, the swan would catch your soul in its wings and take it up to heaven . . . singing a swan song as it went . . ."

His words drift away.

"What do you mean, 'swan song'?" I ask. I don't like where this conversation is going or what it seems like Dad is thinking about: swan songs, souls . . . I shake him a little when his eyes start closing again.

"It's the final song," he whispers. "The last thing a dying person is meant to hear . . . not moans of pain, but singing . . . the most beautiful song ever sung."

His fingers relax in mine and he sleeps. I think about the swans flying overhead when Dad fell down in the field. Maybe Dad was meant to die that day, and the swans that were circling were meant to catch his soul.

No.

I swallow down the sudden tightness in my throat, listen to the soft beeping coming from the machine beside his bed. His electric heartbeat.

"Your soul's not going anywhere," I whisper to him. "I won't let it."

When his breathing starts to get heavier, I take my hand carefully out of his and go out to find Mum.

*M*um and Jack are sitting on the plastic fold-down chairs, talking.

"When are we going to Granddad's next?" I ask as I join them, still wondering what Dad meant by "Old Swanson."

Mum turns to me. "We were actually thinking about going there now. Martin should know how your dad is."

Jack stands, letting the chair bang. "But we're getting takeout first," he says. "There's no way I'm eating his food again. I swear that broccoli had mold on it."

Mum doesn't smile, which is odd. Normally she'd laugh about Granddad's cooking.

"Is something up with Dad?" I ask.

She hesitates before shaking her head. "There's nothing new," she replies. "It's just this operation he's got to have, it's pretty serious. I've been talking to Dad's surgeon and . . ."

She swallows quickly.

"What?" I say.

"It seems there's no guarantee that Dad will survive it."

It feels like someone's kicked me in the stomach. I'm suddenly gasping for air. Mum reaches out to me.

"Hey," she murmurs. "Dad's strong and fit, you know that. I'm probably just worrying too much. I shouldn't have even told you."

Her eyes are digging into mine as if urging me to stop panicking. But it's hard when I can see the fear in her eyes, too. Mum tries to smile it away.

"He'll be OK, Isla," she says. "He's got a great chance, even the surgeon said. So we shouldn't be worried, either. I thought we'd go and tell Granddad anyway, though. It might prompt him to visit."

I look up at Jack, but already he's jiggling his legs, just wanting to move. I walk to the car in a daze. Suddenly, I don't want to go to Granddad's, don't even care about Old Swanson. I want to stay in that hospital room with Dad and never have to leave. I fling myself onto the backseat, not even bothering with a seat belt. Mum doesn't notice, she just sighs loudly as it starts raining again. I watch the drips slide down the window, almost as if they are racing each other. Somehow it seems right that it's raining now. None of us talk. Jack stares straight ahead through the windshield, and the flashes of car lights in front reflect on his skin.

There is a small strip of shabby-looking shops before Granddad's house that we've never stopped at before. The only takeout is Indian.

"Granddad will just have to deal with it," Mum says, catching Jack's look. We all know that Granddad doesn't eat takeout, apart from fish-and-chips.

Mum and Jack go in, but I stay in the car. I turn onto my back and listen to the rain drumming on the roof. Outside I can hear kids squealing as they jump in the puddles. There's a man's voice, too, telling the kids to come inside. Dad would never have done that. When we were younger, Dad was always outside, jumping in the puddles with us.

When Mum and Jack return, they bring smells of garlic and fish and damp clothes.

"We got you dal," Jack says. He chucks a bag of popadams at me and I sit up to catch them. "But if Granddad doesn't like his curry, you'll have to swap."

"He's got cod curry and chips," Mum explains. "Thought that might be close enough."

The rain gets heavier. Someone gathers up the puddle-jumping kids and ushers them into the corner store. Jack reaches down into one of the plastic bags at his feet and tears off a bit of naan bread. He offers me some, but I can't eat. I'm thinking too much about Dad lying in his hospital bed, imagining him being wheeled away to his operation in a few days' time. Will he come back? Mum rubs the sides of her forehead in slow, circular movements. It's what she always does before she gets a headache.

As we pull back onto the highway, Jack turns on the radio. It's still tuned to Mum's talk station. A man with a deep, boring voice is droning on about bird flu.

"The illness has already killed thirty-five people in India," he's saying. "Experts warn of it spreading to epidemic proportions."

I try to block it out. I'm sure this is the last thing any of us want to listen to. But for some reason, Jack doesn't change it. He just drums his fingers against the dashboard. When the man starts talking about a suspected new outbreak in Bangladesh, Mum pushes the windshield wipers to a faster speed. Jack reaches back to grab a popadam.

"Why didn't you see Dad yesterday?" he asks me.

I don't answer him. I feel bad enough as it is about missing Dad, I don't need him to make me feel worse. But Jack doesn't let up.

"Were you seeing that boy again? The cancer kid?" There's something nasty about the way he says it.

"Well, you were playing soccer," I mutter.

Jack's eyes narrow, and I can see him thinking of something to get at me further.

"Is he your boyfriend?"

"Don't be stupid."

I grab the bag of popadams and chuck them at his face.

They smack hard against his chin. He won't give up now. He leans over the seat toward me.

"So you chose to see some sick boy over visiting Dad?"

"I didn't mean to!"

I launch myself at Jack, try to punch him over the headrest. I thump my fists into his shoulder and kick the back of his seat. As Jack turns to grab my arms, the popadams go flying toward the dashboard. Mum lashes out at Jack, tries to stop him.

"Enough!" she yells.

Jack stops, lets go of me.

"You're such an idiot," I hiss, rubbing my skin.

I wait for Mum to tell him off. I look at her when she doesn't. Normally when Jack and I fight, she's the first to react. She can shout louder than everyone in the family put together. But not tonight. Tonight she's like a robot, staring straight ahead and tuning us out. Jack follows my gaze and notices her expression, too. He turns back to the front slowly, and shuts up.

Mum turns up the volume on the radio. I press one ear against the cold window, but I can still hear every word. The man is interviewing someone about how bird flu killed her husband. They cut to the sound of swans honking. I think they're a flock of whoopers. There's the sound of a gun going off. Another swan honking. The flap of wings. I don't want to listen. I want to open my window and let the words and noises escape, but it's still raining outside. I'm about to lean forward to turn the radio down myself when I notice Mum's face.

It's all crumpled-looking. And there are tears on her cheeks. I freeze, just watching. I don't know whether Mum's upset about Dad, or the news report, or about Jack and me fighting. I almost lean forward and grab her hand, but she seems so separate from us, almost as if she's driving in a different car. I glare at the back of Jack's head, wanting him to say something. He's the older brother, after all. But none of us do. We drive the rest of the way to Granddad's in silence.

*G*randdad picks out pieces of fish and wipes the curry sauce off them. He smells each forkful before he puts it into his mouth.

"Do you want the rest of mine?" I say, pushing my plate toward him.

His forehead only wrinkles in annoyance. Mum waits until we're all quiet.

"Graham's going in for a valve transplant," she says. "It's pretty serious."

Granddad's eyes flick across to me and then Jack. He chews carefully on the fish.

"Aren't you worried?" Mum asks eventually, her voice harder-sounding than usual. "About your son?"

Granddad swallows his mouthful, runs his tongue over his teeth. "I'm sure he'll pull through, he's a tough lad."

"Maybe so," she says quietly. "But he'd appreciate a visit."

Granddad's face goes red then. For a moment I'm worried he's going to choke. He even starts to cough a little.

"I don't like hospitals," he says.

He's been saying that a lot lately. Mum's not impressed, though. She clatters her knife and fork onto her plate and glares at him.

"You know," she starts, "Beth's illness was serious, Martin. It wasn't the hospital's fault she died."

Jack exchanges a look with me, and I know what he's thinking. No one mentions Nan in front of Granddad anymore; we all know how upset he gets. But Mum doesn't wait for him to react, she just grabs his plate and storms into the kitchen. He blinks at us, his jaw pulsing at the sides.

Mum scrapes the rest of Granddad's meal into the garbage, then starts to do the dishes really loudly. Glasses and plates clink together as she thumps them all onto the drying rack. Jack leans backward on his chair.

"Want a hand?" he calls out to her.

He just wants to get away, like I do. But Mum doesn't answer. Jack slowly pulls his chair back from the table and goes over to the TV. He channel surfs. Granddad feeds the rest of the popadams to Dig. He doesn't look at any of us, but I see the popadams shake as he holds them out.

Jack settles on some American sitcom, where there are beautiful girls and guys arguing in a restaurant. It's exactly what Granddad wouldn't want. He flinches when the canned laughter comes on. What makes it worse is that Jack starts to laugh, too, at all the really unfunny parts. It's not Jack's normal laugh; I think he's forcing himself to enjoy it. Granddad grips the table so tightly his knuckles go white. He's so tense now that he's starting to look unwell. I lean toward him, try to get his attention.

"Dad said there was some stuff in your barn," I say cautiously. "Things that might be useful for a school project I'm doing. He said something about Old Swanson?"

Granddad looks over at me, his face still red. "Did he?" He keeps frowning. "Beth would never let me throw that old thing away."

I shut up then. The last thing I wanted to do was bring up Nan again. Granddad scrapes his chair back.

"You're welcome to it, though," he mutters, walking away from me. "I suppose it's all just a pile of old rubbish now."

He flicks a glare at Mum in the kitchen and heads toward his sunroom. He shuts the door behind him and stands in the dark. I sit by myself at the table, listening to all the unfunny lines from the TV. Then I grab my coat from the back of my chair. I shut the back door behind me and lean against it for a moment. I take a deep breath of the cold air, then walk carefully down to the barn. It's got dark since we arrived, and the only light to see by is the moon. I draw back the cold, rusty bolt that fastens the large metal doors. It's even darker inside. There could be anything, or anyone, hiding in the blackness. I run my hand along the wall, my fingers scraping on rough wood, and find the light switch.

Lit up, the barn is suddenly huge. I'd forgotten how big it is. There's still a row of stables to one side that used to be part of Granddad's vet practice, but there's just a couple of old, rusty bikes leaning up in them now. The rest of the barn is jammed with crates and furniture and old farm equipment. Lopsided heaps of magazines and books. Sagging boxes. Stuff Granddad no longer wants. Dirt and memories. I have no idea where to start looking. Nothing seems to have anything to do with birds or flying machines. I almost give up. But I don't want to go back to the house yet, either.

I pick a path through the debris and find a box labeled *Graham's School Books and Photographs*. I don't recognize the handwriting, so it must be Nan who wrote it. I trace my fingertips over her letters and try to remember her. She was smiley and energetic, like Dad, and she'd always greet us at the door with the smell of something cooking in the kitchen. It was always fun, coming here, there was always so much to do. Dad used to drive us over all the time. Before Dad, it was Nan who used to tell me stories about the swans. I suppose I miss her, just like Granddad does, although my memory of her is patchy and blurred.

I can remember how she died, though. She had something wrong with her heart, too, like Dad. She'd gone into the hospital, and she never came out. When Dad got the phone call from the hospital to tell him, he turned pale and clung on to the receiver for ages.

I lift the lid off the box and look at the loose photographs inside. There is a picture of Nan in a flowery dress, and a picture of a younger and taller Granddad standing next to a horse. There are pictures of Dad, too. One photograph is so crinkled and thin it could almost be a piece of tracing paper. Dad looks really young in that photo, but he's got the same brownish-blondish hair that he still has now and there are a pair of binoculars around his neck. There's a hand on his shoulder, belonging to someone just out of shot. Granddad, maybe. Dad's smiling as if he's having the best day of his life.

I walk on. Farther down the barn is a dusty steel operating table and a model of a horse skeleton. I touch the cool, plastic bones.

Then I see it. It has to be what Dad meant. It has to be Old Swanson.

I walk toward it. Its eyes stare back at me, unblinking. I crouch down and touch its glass cabinet, wipe away some of the dust. I can remember this now; it used to give me nightmares when I was young. I used to dream of it coming alive and chasing after me through the barn.

It's only stuffed. I can still remember Nan's voice, too, as she explained it to me. She'd laughed and cradled me to her. *This bird's not going to be chasing anyone, that I can promise you.* She'd placed it back into the shadows of the barn. *Silly old useless thing,* she'd murmured. I'd loved Nan so much then.

But Old Swanson looks different than how I remember, less scary somehow . . . more just like the kind of stuffed animal you'd find in a museum. I trace the outline of the wings on the walls of the glass container. I can tell by the large black beak that it's a male mute swan, or was. Its wings are outstretched and pinned to the back of the cabinet, mid-wingbeat. They're huge, beautiful. Its glass eyes aren't creepy in the way l remember. They just look lifeless and sad.

I wonder how I could use this for my project. Perhaps I could attach some wooden planks to the bird's body and make a kind of hang glider with wings instead of sails. It's a bit odd, but it might look something like those da Vinci sketches. And Mrs. Diver would love it.

The cabinet screeches as I drag it along the floor. I rest it against the edge of the old operating table. Then my head turns as I hear Mum yelling for me. She's outside, on the path to the barn. I hear her quick footsteps near the door. I stand up straight, waiting for her. She blinks as she steps inside, looks confused until she finds me.

"Come on, it's time to go," she calls over.

So I give up on the stuffed swan. For now.

I dream of wings that night, huge, powerful white wings. I dream they flap all around me, hundreds of them, beating around my head and body, touching my skin and clothes. They beat so fast that a cyclone whirs up around me. My hair fans backward. I shut my eyes against the wind and the cold. And I spin off into the night, held up by all those feathers.

The first thing I see is Harry's shirt. I've left it on the back of my chair, ready to return to him. I get up and hunt around for one of my own school shirts, but I've used them all. They're sitting in the clothes basket downstairs. Doing the laundry was always Dad's job. Since he's been gone, none of us have even been near the washing machine.

I pull Harry's shirt off the chair. Can I get away with it? I thread my arms through its sleeves, tuck it deep into my pants. I don't have anything else, so I'll have to. I hang my school tie loosely around my neck. Then cover it all with my spare school sweater.

As I go down the stairs, I realize that I like having Harry's shirt on. It makes me feel different somehow. When he gave it to me, I thought it might be weird to wear a sick boy's shirt. But it isn't. It kind of feels like I'm hiding a secret, a nice one. It still smells faintly of pine needles. And him. I brush at my muddy pants as I go into the kitchen, try to pick off some of the worst patches. Jack's already there, shoveling down his breakfast.

"You're in a hurry," I say.

"Playing soccer before school. Meeting the others."

"Can I come?" I say it without meaning to, before I even know why I'm asking. Already I can see him trying to work out how to say "no" to me nicely.

I sit down opposite him, pour myself a bowl of Rice Krispies. I tip the milk in and mix everything around until I can hear the Krispies crackle.

"Why do you always want to come?" he asks. He's suspicious now, looking at me funny.

I stir my spoon through the cereal. "I dunno." I think of his friends sitting together at the playground, the way they always seem so tight. I think of Crowy. "No real reason."

Jack shoves his last mouthful in, then clatters his spoon into the bowl. He sighs as he looks at me. "It's not Crowy, is it? You don't *like* him, do you?"

"Of course not."

I say it too fast. I feel my cheeks go hot and red, and stick a spoonful of Krispies into my mouth so I don't have to say any more. Jack notices, though.

"Ha! Knew it!" He throws his arms up into the air. "What is it with that guy?" He frowns as he tries to figure it out.

Then he gets up from the table, turns as he has another thought. "So it's not just sick boys you like, then?"

On the way to the sink, he stops to hold his spoon above me, waiting for a bit of milk to drop off and land on my neck. I flinch to the side.

"Get off me!"

"Bird's got a crush," he taunts in an annoying sing-songy voice.

"I don't," I say. Because I don't have a crush on Crowy; at least, I don't think I do . . . no more than any other girl in my school does. Anyway, it's Harry I've been thinking of lately. I turn and snatch the spoon from Jack's hand before he can drip any more milk onto me. "He's just the nicest of your loser friends, that's all."

I fling the spoon toward the sink. Only it doesn't get there. It pings off the countertop and hits a glass, which topples and then starts to fall. Jack dives for it, catches it. Just.

"Hey, didn't mean to make you mad," he says, laughing now. "I just think it's funny. First this sick boy in the hospital, and now Crowy. Settle down, sis!"

He washes the spoon, then comes back to the table. He's smiling, but his eyes are still taunting me.

"I don't like either of them," I say. "Not like that."

Jack raises his eyebrows. I'd hate to know what horrible things he's thinking about me. If Dad were here, he would have told Jack off by now. But Jack just gets up from the table, grabs his schoolbag.

"Don't say anything," I blurt out.

Jack stops, half turns. "So it's true?"

I shake my head quickly. "As if!"

He chuckles as he takes an apple from the fruit bowl. "Go get your own group of friends. Crowy's mine!"

He's smiling as he says it, but it still stings. I pat the Rice Krispies farther into the milk until it all turns into one big, soggy mess. Then I get my sketchbook from my bag and try to draw wings until it's time for Mum to take me to school.

$\mathcal{M}$rs. Diver gives us the whole class to work on our projects. She walks between our desks, checking our progress.

"Once you've completed your studies on paper, you can start on the model," she says. "Remember, it can be based on something real that flies, or you can design a flying machine like da Vinci's. Your models don't need to be big and you can use any material you like."

I think of Old Swanson, and wonder if that's the kind of material Mrs. Diver means. A large stuffed swan hardly seems top of the standard list of art supplies. I lean back in my chair and wonder how to use it. What about the wooden hang glider idea? It wouldn't have wheels and gears, like da Vinci's machines, but it would have wings, and if I got it right it would look pretty amazing. Only it would be huge.

I sketch the swan as I think. I draw her wings outstretched, the way she looked when she ran across the surface of the lake. I think about how her feathers angled into the wind, and try to capture that. Behind me, I can hear Jordan complaining to Mrs. Diver about how hard this project is.

"Imagine how hard it was for Leo," she tells him. "He was doing this kind of stuff over five hundred years ago."

I stick my chin into Harry's shirt collar and smell the pine smell. Strange that it should smell so much like trees when Harry seems scared to go outside. I put my sketches of wings aside for a moment and draw a boy's face instead. Two big eyes. It's hard to make them sparkle with an ordinary lead pencil, though. I dot in freckles on the nose, stretch them out across the cheeks. Then I dig my pencil hard into the page until the point snaps. The eyes are too big and the smile is too wide for Harry. And he doesn't look sick enough.

I take a light brown pencil from Sophie's desk and fill in the eyes until they're a chestnut color. I scribble at the hair until it becomes longer and darker . . . a little more like Crowy's. I push away from my desk and look at it. What I've drawn isn't anyone. A bit of Harry, a bit of Crowy, and a bit of someone else entirely. Maybe it's my dream boy. Maybe Jack's right when he says I like them both.

Matt and Jordan start laughing. They're leaning forward over their desks, looking at my picture.

"Who's that?" Matt whispers. "Your boyfriend?"

I instantly cover it up with my hand. But they're hissing

with laughter now, the noise coming through their teeth in breathy gasps.

"You sound like a bunch of snakes," I say.

That only makes them laugh more. I pull a clean sheet of paper over my picture and go back to planning my flying machine. I can't concentrate, though, not now that I know they're watching. I stare at Sophie's page where she's trying to draw an airplane. She sketches out a faint kangaroo design running down its side. The boys are still snickering. I turn my body away from them and stare through the window. The sky is light gray today, like swan feathers. I don't want to be here, not even in art class. I want to be at the lake, running with the swan. I want Harry to come with me.

When the bell rings, I walk down the school corridors still thinking about him. People shove into me as they try to get to their classes, everyone in such a hurry. It's not like the hospital corridors. These corridors are crammed with lockers and schoolbags and laughter. Smells of wet wool sweaters and sweat. At the corner of the corridor, Mr. Symonds, the IT teacher, is waiting for us. I imagine Harry's standing there also, waiting for me like how he waited near Dad's ward.

In IT, I forget about spreadsheets and whatever we're supposed to be doing. I wait until Mr. Symonds is busy helping someone, then log on to the web. I can toggle back to my spreadsheet document if Mr. Symonds comes close. It's not as if I'm the only one doing it. Most of the others are checking their e-mails, and the boys behind me are searching for taboo sites. I hear them whispering as they click onto something new.

I type "how to make a winged flying machine" into the search engine. There are over fourteen million results. The first things that come up are about making model airplanes. I click on a related search that says "make your own wings." These results are more practical, giving me instructions and patterns. I click on a link that shows how someone made huge angel wings using two bags of turkey feathers, and then wore them to a party. But there is nothing about swan wings, and nothing about how to turn stuffed swan wings into a moving model about flight.

I keep clicking.

On the ninth page, I find something different. The picture that comes up is of a pencil-sketched man holding his arms straight out to the sides. Behind him, attached to his arms and chest with what looks like some sort of harness, are huge white wings. Swan's wings. They have to be. They're too big to be anything else. It looks like they're coming right out of his back. I lean close to the computer screen to see. The picture looks ancient and faint, as if it were drawn long before the Internet existed. It looks like something da Vinci could have drawn himself. I scroll down. Below the picture is a list of materials and, below that, instructions.

1. *Acquire the wings of a large bird.*
2. *Bend stainless steel wire into shapes that follow the contours of the wings.*
3. *Make twenty small incisions in the skin along the wing bones . . .*

The instructions get more complicated as I read through. I squint at the diagrams. They seem to show that, once finished, these wings would be able to twist and flap just like a real bird's. Leather straps lead out from a harness and fasten the wearer's arms to the wings so that he can turn them just by moving his body. I keep scrolling through the pages of instructions. They look so hard: too hard for me. But I have Granddad's stuffed swan. And Granddad has loads of weird things in his barn that might help. Perhaps it's possible. I save this link. I minimize the browser and go back to my spreadsheet. When it comes to printing what I've done, I print these instructions, too.

On Saturday Mum drops me at the hospital, then drives off to run some errands.

"I'll meet you at Dad's ward in an hour," she says. "Don't you dare be late."

I thread my way through the parking lot to the fence. I walk quickly through the trees. I'm certain the swan must have flown away by now. But she's still there. Still alone, too.

I drop my bag and go right up to the water's edge. The swan keeps watching me, waiting for me. I've told Mum I want to sketch her wings again, but that's not the only reason I'm here. I tighten my shoelaces. I start to jog and wait for her to follow. It's not long before I hear her feet slapping on the water behind. This time, I try something different. I slow down. I glance at her and see that she's slowing, too. I speed up. She does the same, rising onto the water's surface and beating her wings. I stop abruptly. She does, too.

She sticks her feet out in front of her like brakes, making water shoot up around her, then waits for my next move. She's doing exactly what I do. *Exactly*.

I turn to her, suddenly fed up with all this weirdness.

"Stop following me!" I yell. I run toward the water, waving my arms back and forth. "Why won't you just fly?"

She flinches, but doesn't move back. She stares at me blankly, looking at me first from one side and then turning her head and looking from the other. She blinks. I pick up a stone from near my feet and skim it across the water. I don't know why I do it; I suppose I just want her to react like a normal bird. But she doesn't move away and the stone sinks before it reaches her. She waits a moment, then swims toward me. She steps onto the bank. Totally unafraid.

Her head is low and submissive. So I walk right up to her. It's as if she wants me to touch her. I hold out my hand, then rest it against her head. She doesn't move back. I take a deep breath and force my shoulders to relax.

"Why aren't you scared?" I say, calmer now.

I stroke her neck, feeling her thin body beneath the feathers. She's unbelievably soft. And so still. She shuts her eyes and I touch the tiny, yellowish feathers around them. I sigh out, sit down opposite her.

"You're just stupid, aren't you? A head case of a swan. Maybe I should tell someone to stick you in a zoo."

I'm exhausted, frustrated by trying to figure her out. There's a flicker of morning sunlight dancing across my face, making me sleepy. After a while, the swan inches back into the water. She digs her beak into the wall of the bank and starts feeding. Just a normal bird. I lean up against the tree stump and look across the lake, absently counting the birds. Three mallards, two tufted ducks, four coots.

The day gets brighter. Soon the sun has burst through the clouds and is bouncing onto the lake. It makes the water shimmer. Makes it hard to watch. I shut my eyes, enjoying the warmth against my skin. It feels like it's the first bit of sun we've had since summer. It feels special.

I concentrate on the warmth, try not to think about Dad and the hospital and everything bad. The insides of my eyelids are pink from the bright light. I try to make my body as still as the tree stump I'm leaning against. And soon, I feel my thoughts drifting away.

36

I feel myself sinking . . . It's as if I'm falling down into the earth, being pulled toward the ground. The wind is whooshing at my ears.

Then the images come. Everything flutters at first. There are so many pictures, all flashing into my brain so quickly. I try to grasp at them. And slowly, I begin to see.

There's sky. Clouds. A whir of wings. Swans are all around me. I look down and see the whole world stretched out below me.

I'm flying.

There's a hint of a lake ahead. Swans start murmuring as we get closer. There's a wind, pushing from behind . . . pushing me forward.

It happens so quickly.

The swan in front twists backward, screeching. He looks around as he starts to fall, his wings useless and still. I turn, try to find a different route. The wind is too strong. Another bird screams.

Suddenly, I see them. There are two lines across the sky, blocking our path. I feel the flock splitting, losing formation. Scattering. I fly straight at the sun, and hope. I hear a sharp smack as another bird hits the lines. I keep beating. I twist my body, try to get a grip on the wind. The birds flying with me begin to drop away. But I can't stop. Not yet. Not until I'm far away. I look down at the land as I go.

And far, far below, there are two people. A big one and a small one. A cold gust whips around me as I realize it's me down there! Me and Dad. We're on a path, at the edge of a lake, and we're waving our arms madly, yelling out.

It's what we were doing that first day, the day when the swans arrived.

My eyes snap open. The swan is still drifting on the lake in front of me, still digging her beak into the bank and feeding. She's not looking at me at all. But it was her story I was dreaming, I'm sure of it. I crawl toward her. Her head comes up as she checks where I am, then goes down again to feed. She drifts farther away. She couldn't look more like an ordinary bird if she tried. I rub my eyes. Check the time on my watch. It's still early. I've only been asleep for about ten minutes, but already the sun's disappeared behind a cloud, making the lake look so much darker. I glance back at the swan, but she's floating farther away, only intent on eating. I don't want to sketch her. Not now. I just want to talk to Harry.

I get to his room in a daze. It feels like I'm still half asleep, still flying high above the preserve . . .

The same nurse lets me in.

"He looks worse than he is," she tells me carefully.

Harry's in bed, propped up so he can see out the window. The skin around his eyes looks gray and thin and makes his cheekbones stand out. I hover in the doorway at first. He squints as he focuses on me and I can see he's not totally with it. Then I sit on the edge of his bed, close to him.

"I was watching you," he says.

I smile. I'm glad. I reach for the glass of water on his bedside table and put it into his hands. "You don't look so good today."

He manages a grimace. "More chemo." He blinks slowly, takes a sip. He pushes the glass back into my hand. "Help me sit up."

He reaches out to me. I look at his smooth, pale hands. His long fingers. I lean toward him and he grabs me around my shoulders. Carefully I put my hands around his chest. My face is near his neck. He doesn't smell sick: He smells like trees and life. I wonder if he can feel my breath on his skin. He pushes down on my shoulders, his fingers cold through my shirt, pushes himself up. He shuffles back against the pillows. I almost want to stay like that a moment longer, buried into his body, but I don't. Both of us look away as I take my arms back.

"Now," he says, once he's settled, "what's been going on?"

He nods toward the window, really wanting to know. I tell him how the swan was following my movements exactly. I tell him how I fell asleep and dreamed about her flock flying into the lines. I watch his face as he listens. He doesn't laugh or look doubtful. Even if he doesn't believe me, he's making a good effort of pretending to.

He yawns slowly. "Maybe you should find her flock," he says. "Maybe if she had her flock, she'd fly."

It's a good thought, but I start laughing all the same. "How would I get a swan to a flock?" I say. "Taxi?"

He smiles slightly. "Yeah, it is kind of stupid, I guess."

I look back out the window. I can still see her there, floating alone.

"It's probably fine," I tell Harry. "Whooper swans won't migrate back to Iceland for at least another three months, so there's time. Time for her to start flying again. Time for her flock to find her, too. I don't know why I'm so worried about her, really."

When I look back at Harry, his eyes are shut. He looks so much more relaxed now that he's slipping into sleep. His hair is definitely getting thinner: I can see patches of skin on his head, and there are gingery strands all over his blankets. His breathing becomes heavier as I watch. I move my hand across the bed and touch his fingers. They're still so cold, like Dad's hands in the ambulance. I think about holding Harry's hand in mine, making him warm again.

I wait there for a little while, wondering if he'll wake up.

When he doesn't, I write him a note on the back of a flyer for the hospital cafeteria.

Keep watching her. Text me if anything changes. Isla

I leave my number at the bottom. I don't know whether to add an x after my name. I look at his pale white skin, his fluttering eyelids covering up those bright eyes underneath. He looks like one of those stone angels you find in churches sometimes. I don't know why, but I lean forward and brush a bit of hair from his cheek. His skin twitches. I move my hand away instantly. I don't know what I'd do if he woke up and found me touching his face. I hold my breath, waiting. But he doesn't move again. He's already too deep in sleep to even notice.

*M*um and Jack are waiting on the chairs outside Dad's ward. As I look at their faces, my stomach sinks.

"What happened?"

Mum reaches for my hand. "His heartbeat has sped up again," she says. "They're moving up his operation."

"Is he OK?"

Mum nods. "Go in and see him, babe. Jack and I will wait here."

I go in alone. Dad's eyes are closed, and he's really still. I can't stop swallowing as I watch him. After a moment, I hold my hand out. Place it down onto his chest. I spread my fingers wide to try and feel. And there, just faintly, is a heartbeat. That quick, unsteady beat is the best feeling in the world.

I breathe out. I keep my hand there, resting on his chest.

I don't want to pull it away. I stay really still, just feeling the soft thuds.

I try to pass a thought to Dad, a kind of prayer to make him better. His eyelids flicker as if he's heard me in his mind. I sit on the edge of the chair beside his bed and wait. When his eyes open, I lean over him. His mouth twitches into a smile as he focuses on me.

"How's that swan?" he murmurs, breathless again. "Still there?"

I nod. "She won't fly."

"No flock, either?"

"Not yet."

He frowns.

"Don't worry," I say. "There's still ages before they migrate."

"I suppose." But he keeps frowning.

I lean closer to him. "She'll fly," I tell him. "Any day now."

And Dad's mouth twitches to a smile again.

*I*t's Indian takeout again. And a trip to Granddad's. Mum gets him the only proper English meal on the menu: omelet-and-chips.

"I don't know why I'm even bothering," she says as she drives. "It's not as if he'll appreciate our visit."

I lean forward to rest my head on the back of her seat. "But I want to go," I say.

Jack grunts and sticks his feet up on the dashboard. "Just because *you* do doesn't mean we all do."

Mum leans across to slap his feet away. "He's your grand-dad, Jack!"

"But it's Saturday night!" He closes his hand into a fist and rests it against the window.

Granddad's expecting us this time, and he's got plates already laid out on the table. "All right, Cath?" he says, taking the bags from her.

Mum raises her eyebrows in surprise and follows him to the table. "Graham's operation is on Monday now," she says quietly. "They've moved it up."

Granddad keeps his head down, focusing on taking all the containers out of the bags. "So, the ticker is getting quicker?" he says. His eyes dart over to me and Jack, and then he starts laughing at his joke.

Mum's lips tense into a thin line. She takes the containers from the middle of the table and thumps them onto our plates. "Glad you find your son's illness funny," she mutters.

Jack slops his curry onto his plate and starts shoveling it in. I chase an onion strand around with my fork. I'm not hungry. I just want to eat quickly so I can be out in the barn. Granddad looks at us again before he leans toward Mum.

"Those kids are petrified," he says quietly. "You don't need to worry them unnecessarily about Graham."

"And what would you do? Not tell them anything?" Mum's eyes bore into Granddad's. He looks down immediately.

Neither of them notices as Jack slopes off to the couch. I suck up a long, thin strand of spinach and think about joining him. I rub my lips together, feeling the grease there. Mum and Granddad start talking about what happened to Nan for the fifty-billionth time.

"It wasn't Graham's fault that she died in the hospital," Mum says, raising her voice a little.

I put my knife and fork neatly together on the plate, drag my chair out quietly, and slip away from the table. I walk to the barn, sticking my hands deep into my coat pockets. The pages I printed out in IT are there, folded up neatly. I pull back the bolt, flick on the light, and walk straight to the stuffed swan. A door slams somewhere. I don't know whether it's to do with the argument or the wind. I listen to hear if anyone's coming looking for me, but it's quiet again immediately after. I touch the glass surrounding the swan, make a line through the dust as I trace his wings. It would be brilliant to have wings, to be able to fly away whenever you needed to. Birds have it easy like that.

I take the instructions out of my pocket. I glance over the long equipment list: *one large bird, leather, strong rope, buckles and belts, knife, stiff thread* . . . I look at the diagrams that show how to cut the wings, how to thread wire through them and make them move. Then I look at the diagrams that show how to make the leather harness in the middle. It looks so complicated. If Dad were here, he'd be able to do it so easily. I think of him lying in his hospital bed, all alone and waiting, with us all here at Granddad's.

I go looking for equipment. I find a black plastic box with a whole lot of knives and clamps and clipper things inside. It must be stuff Granddad used in his vet practice. I pick up the box and go back to the swan cabinet. I lay it facedown against the concrete. There are small metal fasteners attaching the backing to the frame. I use pliers to get them loose, then grip the backing and pull. It's heavier than I thought because the stuffed swan is attached to it, but I manage to lift it out. I turn it over, put it on the floor, and look down at the huge white bird at my feet. It's so massive, stretched out like that. I run my hands over its spread wings. They're so soft, but springy and tough, too. And so wide. I remember what Dad said about swans' wings catching souls and carrying them to heaven, and I think I can understand why people thought that. If anything could carry something precious, they could.

I take a small, sharp knife and slit the tight loops of string that fasten the swan to the backing. The wings flop backward when I've finished, bigger than ever. I smooth them out, then run my hands down to the place where the wings join the body. It's firm there, as if there are still muscles pressed up against the feathers. I think about the knife hacking through them all, ripping them apart. I sit back onto my heels. I don't know if I can do this. It would be like chopping up a bird, destroying something beautiful.

There's a thud. Then footsteps, thumping heavily on the path outside. I freeze, the knife still in my hand. I don't know why I should feel guilty about what I've been doing, but I do. Should I try to hide it?

Jack comes storming in as I stand up. He doesn't even look at me, just kicks a cardboard box so it goes skidding across the concrete.

"Stupid Mum." He boots a pile of junk, sending a plastic plant pot into a corner. "Can't she just accept that Granddad's not going to visit Dad? She's driving me nuts!" He sends another plastic pot in the same direction as the first. Then he looks at me. "Why are you in here, anyway?" He flinches when he sees what's in my hand. "What are you doing with that?"

He's looking at the knife that I'd forgotten to leave with the swan. His eyes flick back to my face and he's staring at me as if I'm some sort of psychopath.

"Nothing," I say.

But he doesn't believe me. He walks toward me, grabs my arms. Turns them over.

"I'm not trying to hurt myself, Jack!"

I wrench my arms away from him, put the knife back in my coat pocket. Jack's eyes flash to where I was sitting with Swanson.

"Show me," he demands. I don't move for a moment, but he steps up closer and says firmly, "Show me what you're doing."

I don't argue with him. What would be the point? Besides, maybe he can help me understand some of the complicated instructions.

"I've seen this thing before," he says when I take him to the swan. "I remember it from when we were young." He lifts the swan away and the wings hang down over his arms. "Why have you taken it out of its case?"

I show him the instructions. He reads them quickly, his eyes squinting at the small text. He looks back at the swan, brushes his fingers against the section where the wing joins the body.

"You're going to cut it up? Why?"

I shrug. "Just an art project."

"You're crazy." He snickers. "You won't chop up a bird in a million years, even if it is stuffed. Give me the knife."

He holds his hand out. He glares at me, challenging me.

When I don't give him the knife, he stands and scuffs his shoe against one of the wings.

"Don't, Jack!"

I know he's only angry because of what he's heard in the house, but it makes my fingers tense around the knife all the same.

"I'll do it," I say.

I crouch with the knife hovering above the bird's right shoulder. I bring it down until it touches the feathers. I press gently, testing to see how hard I need to push. Jack kneels down, too.

"You won't," he whispers.

Something snaps inside me then. I turn from the swan to push him away. I hold the knife up toward him.

"Just get lost!" I say. "Go and be angry somewhere else."

Jack's sneer drops immediately. He holds his hands up in defense. "Hey, calm down," he mutters. "I was only trying to help."

"You're not helping," I say. "You're just making everything worse." I glare at him. I keep the knife clenched in my fist until he gets up from the floor.

Jack takes a couple of steps away, looking at me like I'm mental. I don't care. He can think whatever he wants as far as I'm concerned. I turn back to the swan, wrap both of my hands around the knife, and thrust it down.

There's a ripping sound as it goes in. I grit my teeth and push harder. I push until the blade clinks against the floor on the other side. Then I hack down, pulling the knife in jerky movements to make it go through all the stuffing. I shut my eyes so I don't have to think about it too much. I keep going until the whole wing is chopped off.

Only then do I open my eyes. There are chunks of stuffing everywhere, all over the wings and floor. All over me, too. The separated wing reminds me of the one at the preserve that the fox didn't eat. It makes me feel slightly sick. I wipe the blade on my jeans to get rid of all the bits of stuffing. Then I drag the swan's body back toward me and get started on the other wing. I try to pretend it's just a pillow I'm cutting into, not a shoulder. Not something that used to be alive.

When I look up again, Jack's gone. I sit back. Focus on the strands of cobwebs linking the rafters in the roof. I take one deep breath, then another, then rest my head on my knees. The knife clatters as it drops to the floor and I can feel tears stinging my eyes. I hug my knees to my face and let them come.

*T*he barn gets colder. A wind starts battering at its metal sides. The fluorescent light above me flickers. After a while, I crawl forward on my hands and knees, through the bits of stuffing. I pile the two wings on top of each other and put them to one side, then make myself lift the body. It feels so long and thin, and it's so much lighter without its wings attached, like lifting a pillow. I don't know where to put it, so I lay it on the old operating table. I stretch it out like a corpse and turn its face away from me.

I sit next to the wings and pick up the instructions. A part of me doesn't want to keep going. But the other part of me is stubborn and can't leave the wings like this: all chopped up and useless. It feels wrong somehow, a waste. I ignore the really complicated instructions about how to make the leather harness and instead follow the ones that tell me to make a series of slits along the wings. I dig the knife in quickly but carefully, then get up and start sifting through the boxes, looking for wire to thread through the cuts.

I hear the barn door open again. Granddad steps in cautiously. Tries a smile. It's obviously fake, put on to pretend that everything's OK now between him and Mum.

"Your mum's asking if you want to go home," he says.

I wonder if he can tell I've been crying. He steps toward me and I see his eyes widen as he clocks the swan's body on the operating table. He frowns as he sees the wings, too. He looks at me a little like Jack did, as if he thinks I'm going mad.

I brace myself as he comes closer, ready for him to be angry because I chopped up something that reminds him of Nan. I wait for his face to turn red and scary-looking. Suddenly, I wish Jack had stayed. I try to explain about making a model for my art project. And he stops and looks down at the wings, his face not frowning anymore.

His joints click as he kneels. "All this effort for a school project?"

"I want to give it to Dad, too," I say. "When I've finished."

It's the first time I've said it out loud, but I do want that.

Granddad holds out his hands and I give him the instructions. I don't go on and tell him how I'm hoping, stupidly, that these wings will make Dad feel better, too. I look up at the light, watch the dust particles floating in front of it. When I look back at Granddad, I have tiny stars dancing before my eyes. He takes his glasses out of his pocket so he can read the instructions better. Then he lifts one of the wings, making a noise in his throat that sounds like a mixture of a laugh and a cough.

"I never imagined you'd want Swanson so you could chop him up," he mutters. "He's been sitting here for years."

I tense, still waiting for him to be angry. But instead there's that small coughlike chuckle again. He seems kind of amused. He turns back to the wing and examines the slits I've made there.

"Not bad," he says. "It wouldn't take much to stitch all that up. A few more cuts here . . ."

I crouch a little closer to him. "You're not angry?" I say. "That I chopped it up?"

He peers at me over his glasses, his eyes wider than I've ever seen them.

"Why would I be?" His voice is low and gravelly. "Your nan wondered what to do with this bird for years."

He picks up the instructions again, reads them slowly. "I've got most of that equipment. Even got an old climbing harness of your father's somewhere around here. We could use that instead of making our own."

He peers at the diagram that shows how to attach strips of leather to the wings and wrap them around the wearer's body.

"It's for you to wear, yes?"

I shrug. "I s'pose."

"Your father's old climbing harness would fit, then."

The wrinkles in his forehead disappear for a moment as he thinks about it. He looks so much like Dad then that I can't help gasping. He gets up slowly and shuffles back to the boxes around the operating table. He finds one that has loads of useful stuff, including the strong thread he used for stitching animals.

He finds the harness that Dad once used for rock climbing and turns it over, checking for damage.

"Your dad used to climb everything," he explains. "Even when he was younger, he was a bit of a daredevil, a bit of a fool."

He gives it to me to hold. I pull at the straps. It's smaller than the harnesses Dad uses now to chop branches down for work, and it would fit me perfectly.

"We just need to run some more material and straps up the back so we can fasten it around your chest," Granddad murmurs, turning it to show me. "And attach it to the wings, of course."

He's nodding quickly as he looks at it, his expression no longer like the grumpy old man everyone argues with. So I let him help. It's weird, but he seems to change a bit as he does. He smiles more and his voice gets softer. For a moment, I can almost pretend that it's Dad here with me.

His eyes squint as he chooses a needle and tries to thread it.

"I'll help," I say, and do it for him.

Then he begins to stitch. He works quickly and carefully, not damaging the structure of the swan's wings at all.

"Did you know," he murmurs, "that the bones in a swan's wing are pretty much the same as the bones in a human arm? Isn't that amazing? A few people even argue that our bodies have descended from birds."

By the time he asks me for the next instruction, there's a small smile on his face.

When Mum gets there, Granddad is still stitching thread through the wings. Granddad doesn't turn to acknowledge her and she doesn't say anything to him, either. Instead she finds an old coat, spreads it out next to me, and sits down. Her eyes slowly take in the whole big wingspan of the swan.

"Jack said you were making something for school," she says.

"And for Dad."

She nods. "They're beautiful."

It's not long before Jack comes in, too. His eyes widen when he sees what we've done.

"I can't believe you actually did it," he says, then sprawls out on the other side of Granddad and starts fiddling with the box of surgical equipment.

I wait for Mum to tell me it's time to go. But she just watches quietly. So I help Granddad with the climbing harness, holding it still for him to sew the wings to. His stitches are so small and neat, I can hardly see them.

"You're good at that," I say.

"Just practice."

His hands aren't even shaking. Now that he's helping me with this, he seems like a different person. Mum's noticed, too, I'm sure.

After a while, Jack starts sighing and looking at his watch. "They'll all be waiting for me," he says. "Can we go now?"

Mum leans on my shoulder as she pushes herself up. "Come on, Isla, it's almost nine."

Granddad stops threading the needle, a flash of frustration across his face.

"I want to keep going," I say, suddenly having an idea. "I want this ready for Dad to see before his operation."

Mum fiddles with her rings as she thinks.

"I could drop her back at the house," says Granddad. "Or even drop her straight at the hospital tomorrow morning."

I look quickly at Granddad; we all do. It's so unlike him to suggest something helpful. For a moment or two, it doesn't look like Mum knows what to say. She raises her eyebrows at me.

"It's up to you, babe."

I nod, thinking of Dad . . . wanting to try anything right now to make him feel better. Even if it's something as crazy as showing him a flying machine I made. "I want to finish this." And I do. We're so close to the end, it seems crazy to stop now. Even if it does mean that I have to stay at Granddad's again.

Mum brushes her fingers through my hair as she goes. "Be good."

But Granddad and I don't sleep. We keep going for hours, turning the wings, gradually, into a flying model. At some stage, Granddad fetches a lamp from another part of the barn and plugs it in nearby for more light. He gets scratchy old blankets, too, and we wrap them around our shoulders. The dust on them makes my throat itch. After a while, the small letters on the instructions sheet blur before my eyes. I bury my head inside the blankets and just watch Granddad work. He looks so focused, so completely concentrated on getting it right. I wonder if he was like this as a vet. Perhaps this focus and skill is why he thought he could care for Nan at home, why he was so angry when Dad took her to the hospital.

I'm pretty much asleep by the time Granddad leans away from what we've made and notices me. "Come on," he says. "Let's go inside and get a drink."

The wind has died down when we get out of the barn. The only sound is our feet, crunching against the dirt path.

I blink my eyes when we get into Granddad's brightly lit kitchen, and look down at the linoleum floor until they've adjusted.

We sit on the couch sipping tea, sweet and hot. Granddad looks tired, but not exhausted. There's a sparkle in his eyes. But I feel myself sinking down and the cup being taken from my hands. My head drops back into the cushions, springs and feathers beneath me.

And I dream of Dad. Swans are carrying him up into the sky, singing the most beautiful song as they go. It's a swan song to take him higher.

A beeping sound goes off near my ear and I wake with a start. The room is silver gray and Granddad isn't next to me anymore. There's just a cold cup of tea on the carpet, and my phone. I lean over and grab it. The message is from a number I don't recognize.

> Swan tried to fly again, but no luck. Saw a flock flying in the distance, but they didn't land. Harry.
> P.S. Wish you were here.

I read it three times. Then I check the time: 6:47 a.m. He's up early. I lie there, looking around at Granddad's shabby living room, and wonder what to text back. I stretch my arms above my head. My body aches as if I have been running for hours. I sit up and glance over to the kitchen. The house is silent and still, and empty. I get up and open the back door. There's a robin's clear, loud voice. I scan the shadowy fields for swans, stand on my tiptoes and try to see the lake.

I reply to Harry.

I'll see you later. I've got a surprise for you.

I stick the phone in my pocket and walk. I yawn in the crisp, morning air and feel the dampness of dawn on my cheeks. The barn doors are open, and as I get closer I can see Granddad searching through a pile of boxes. He looks up when he hears me.

"I've finished it," he says. "Just now."

"Why didn't you wake me?"

A part of me feels angry. I wanted to finish the flying model; it's my project, after all. But then I see the swan wings stretched out across the concrete, with the climbing harness in between them, and I'm glad Granddad's done it. There are wires connecting different parts of the harness to the feathers. There are Velcro loops running down the middle of each wing for my arms to be attached and gardening gloves toward the wing tips for my hands to go in. The model looks beautiful and complicated and exactly like the picture. I pick up the crumpled instructions and check how Granddad's made it.

"I don't know where you found those instructions," Granddad says slowly. "But they're good. Whatever they say to do just works."

I kneel down to the model. I run my fingers over the thick leather strips that lead up from the back of the harness and see how securely they're attached to the wings.

"This is amazing," I say. "Better than I could have done."

This makes Granddad chuckle. He draws his shoulders back and looks proud of himself. It's the same sort of movement that a swan makes when it resettles its feathers.

"Let's see if they work," he says.

He lifts the wings up carefully, holding them flat. They look absolutely massive.

"Are they heavy?" I ask.

Granddad shakes his head. "Not really. Surprising, eh? But then, it's only stuffing inside this thing."

Granddad helps me step into the climbing harness. I tighten it around my hips. Already I can feel the wings pulling me backward.

"It'll be better in a minute," Granddad says. "Hold your arms out straight."

I do, and he fastens my outstretched arms to the wings by wrapping the Velcro straps tightly around them. Then he passes a leather strap that looks like an old belt around my chest, attaching me to the material running down my back. I breathe in as he tightens another leather strap around my stomach. He closes the final bit of Velcro, securing my hands inside the gardening gloves.

"There," he murmurs. "Nice and snug."

I can see my shadow on the far wall, my tiny-looking body with the huge wings spread out behind me. I look like some sort of winged superhero. Bird Girl. I try moving my fingers, one by one. I look down at the wings, get a little buzz of excitement when I see the wires leading out from the gloves moving, too. I follow the wires with my eyes and notice the primary flight feathers parting and twisting with my movements. I roll my shoulders and feel the feathers ruffle out behind me. It's exactly the way a real bird would move its feathers.

"Magic," Granddad breathes.

The feathers are so close to me that I can smell their dust and stuffing. The wings press against my shoulder blades as if I'm wearing a big backpack. I arch my spine and watch my shadow on the wall; the wings change shape slightly with each movement I make.

"Try folding them inward," Granddad says. He checks the instructions. "Bend your elbows and bring your fists toward you."

I try it. At first the wings seem too stiff to move, but I pull on them a little harder and they fold inward obediently.

"Now try to cross your arms over your chest."

I slide my right arm over my left and the wings settle around me, back in place. Granddad presses his hands across his mouth, shaking his head gently. It's what Dad does when he's really impressed with something.

"Just like a real bird," he murmurs again. "I've never seen anything like it."

I can't do anything but nod. I'm still blown away by it all myself. Granddad and I have made an amazing wing model, an actual flying machine, just like da Vinci's.

"Let's take them to the hospital," I say. "Right now."

"*Y*ou can park over there."

Granddad's hands tighten on the wheel. He doesn't want to park, but I'm making him. He keeps the car running and waits for me to get out. I lean across and turn the key in the ignition.

"Will you come in, show Dad with me?"

Granddad breathes out slowly, then gets out of the car. He doesn't say anything as we walk across the parking lot toward the hospital entrance. His eyes are darting around, though, and he's clasping his hands together tightly. I hold the wing model folded up in a tight bundle, close to my chest. It's still early, not long after eight. Mum won't be here yet; we've arranged to meet outside Dad's ward at nine. I hug the wings tighter as I realize how cold it is. Granddad bumps into me as an ambulance screams past, its lights flashing bright in the misty morning. He hesitates as we go through the entrance hall.

"Are you sure they'll let me in?" he asks.

I shrug. "We'll just wait until they do."

He pauses near the plastic palm trees and I think he's going to turn around and go home right then.

"Think of Dad's face when he sees what we've made," I say.

He keeps following me to the elevators. I hold the doors open until he gets in after me. There's a small boy and his mum already in there and they keep giving me weird looks. I'm sure the boy thinks I'm carrying a real bird. It's actually quite difficult to carry the wing model. I have to put my arms underneath to support it and rest my chin on top. I suppose if you couldn't see the harness underneath it, it would look like I was hugging a swan.

Granddad walks really slowly all the way to Dad's ward. There's a janitor up ahead, mopping the floors, and Granddad turns away from the disinfectant smell. I see how hard this is for him, how much he doesn't want to be here. When we get to the entrance, he stops and folds his arms over his chest.

"Why don't you check that it's OK first?" he mumbles.

I go in and ask the nurse.

"Nine is when visiting hours begin," she says, eyeing the wing model warily. "I'll let you in then."

When I come back out to the corridor, Granddad is gone. I run back the way we've come, but can't find him anywhere. The elevators are all full, so I hold the banister tightly with one hand and keep my other around the wing model as I race down the stairs. I turn sideways at the bottom to get past someone in a wheelchair. Granddad's not waiting in the café, or near the plastic trees. I go through the sliding doors and into the parking lot. He's there, his hand on the car door. He waves when I see him.

"Your dad will love those wings," he calls out to me.

Then he gets into his car. I'm so shocked that he's leaving like this; I just stand in the entrance, right in the way of everyone trying to get in, and stare after his car. I can feel the anger in my throat and chest, making everything tight. I clutch the wing model. I understand now why Mum's always so mad at him.

I turn quickly. I take the elevator to Harry's room instead. There's a lady coming out of the ward as I get there and she holds the door for me. The ward is quiet and sleepy. There aren't even any nurses at the front desk.

Harry's door is closed. I peer in through the glass section of it and see that he's awake. He's sitting up in bed, turned away from me. He's looking out the window through a gap in his curtains. I glance down the corridor to check for nurses. Then I try to put on the harness. It's hard without Granddad there to help, and I can't tighten anything properly. I unfold the wings a little so I can get my arms into the loops, and fasten the Velcro straps with my teeth. I press my legs against Harry's door until it opens. I sidle into his room sideways. Then I uncross my arms, and the wings spread out behind me.

Harry turns. His mouth opens a little as he focuses on me and his eyes go wide as saucers.

"Isla?" he whispers.

I almost laugh at the way he looks so totally gobsmacked. "Who were you expecting?"

I take a step toward him, the wings bouncing lightly around me. It's hard to keep balanced with them outstretched like this, hard to walk straight. They're so huge. My left wing brushes against the TV on the wall, and I try to pull it inward. Everything feels stiff and disjointed, but I'm beginning to get the hang of it. It's actually easier than I thought. Harry raises his hand as if he wants to touch the feathers. I stand close to the bed, and let him. His face is as pale as his pillowcase.

"It looks like you've seen a ghost," I say, trying to joke.

He doesn't smile back. "I thought I had," he says. "With the light from the corridor shining in behind you . . . you looked like an angel."

I laugh at him for real then. "Don't be stupid."

But he's completely serious. He's quiet for a bit, just taking it all in. He strokes his fingers against the wings.

"Where did you get these?" he asks. "What are they for?"

I explain about my art project and flying machines and how I chopped up the stuffed swan. I tell him how Granddad helped.

"He used to be a vet," I explain. "So he's good at sewing stuff."

I show Harry how I can use my fingers to move different parts of the wings. Then I fold them in by crossing my arms over my chest. We experiment with them a bit more and find out that I can move other parts of the wings by twisting my arms. Harry's face gets more and more excited as we discover each new thing.

"They're the most amazing thing ever," he says.

His expression keeps me laughing, and the harness gets tighter against my chest as I do.

Then Harry's expression changes. "I just thought of something," he says. "You said the swan on the lake followed your every move."

"She did. When I ran, she ran . . . when I stopped—"

"So she followed you exactly, did *exactly* what you did?"

I nod. "What are you getting at?"

His smile gets bigger, stretching out into his cheeks. "What if you ran with her with those wings on?"

"What?"

"What if you, or me, found out how swans use their wings to take off, which feathers they move, that kind of thing . . .

and you showed her how to do it with this flying model?"

"Why?"

"If she's following you anyway, then maybe she might follow you doing this, too. You could show her how to take off."

I stare at him. "That's crazy."

"Maybe." He laughs. "Think you can run with that on?"

I pull my wings inward. "It's pretty awkward," I say. "Anyway, I'd never remember how to move these wings and run at the same time."

"What if I came with you? What if I called out instructions as you ran?"

He's got my full attention now. I hold his gaze, testing how serious he is. "You'd come with me?"

He nods slowly. "I'd like to."

"What about your medication? The chemo? I thought you didn't want to go down there."

He keeps looking at me, his skin golden from the light coming in the window.

"If I don't go now, who knows when it will be," he says. "I'm fed up with being careful all the time." He keeps talking, softly and urgently. "We don't even have to tell the hospital. We could go at night."

I hold up my hand, stop him there. I don't want to say it, but I do. "I'm not sneaking you out of here. I'd get in real trouble."

"It's fine; no one's around, nothing ever happens here

at night. I should know, I'm awake most of it."

His voice falters a little when he says that, but he doesn't drop my gaze. He's really serious about this, I can see that. I've no idea why. I let myself imagine what it might be like to be down near the lake with Harry, in the dark. Just us and the swan. But in my imagination, Harry is healthy and strong and leads the way confidently, his hand in mine. In my imagination, he's not sick.

"Aren't you scared?" I ask.

He nods. "Of course."

"Then why do it?" I want to know why he's changed his mind.

"My doctor talked to me yesterday," he explains. "Once they find a match for my bone marrow, they'll put me in isolation. I probably won't be able to see you and I won't be able to leave, and who knows when I'll come out. So, I . . ."

I nod, suddenly understanding. "You want to go while you still can?"

"I want to go with you."

I sit down on his bed. He looks scared and young, not like the Harry I know at all. His hand is near mine on the blankets. I could reach across and touch it.

"I'll think about it," I say.

He nods once, looks back to the window. I wait for a few moments for him to say more. Then I get up from the bed and start taking the wings off. I use my teeth to unfasten the

Velcro around my arms. Harry shuffles over and helps.

"They'll work," he whispers. "I know they will. She'll copy you."

"How do you know?"

He shrugs. "A feeling."

I smile. It's like something Dad would say. He holds the wings while I step out from the harness. I turn back to the bed to bundle them up. I want to brush my hand against Harry's and find out how much he really does like me. But instead, I clutch the wings close to my chest, and take a couple of steps toward the door.

"I bet your dad loves them," he says.

Again his eyes hold mine. And I want, more than anything, to tell him to come with me, down to the lake. I want to say loads of things. But instead I just nod and smile and say:

"Keep watching her."

I walk to Dad's ward. All the while I'm wondering about what Harry suggested. Would it work? If I could make my flying model move like a real swan's wings, would the swan really copy me? Could I teach her to take off? It seems too crazy to even try. But Harry said he'd come with me. He'd see the swan. It's exactly what I'd wanted. So why didn't I agree?

I wait for Mum outside Dad's ward. She smiles when she sees what I've got bundled up in my arms.

"You finished the project, then?"

I nod. "I've brought them for Dad to see."

When we walk past the ward desk, the round Scottish nurse who seems to be in charge puts her hand firmly on my shoulder.

"You want to bring *that* into the ward?" She looks disapprovingly at my flying model.

"The wings are stuffed," I say. "It's for Dad."

She raises her eyebrows at Mum. "Just this once," she says. "But they're not staying." She turns away from us, shaking her head.

Dad's sitting up, waiting. "What's all the fuss out there?" he asks.

I look behind to check that the nurse isn't watching, then place the wing model on Dad's bed. His eyes widen and sparkle. He runs his hand over it slowly, unfolding it to examine the stitching.

"This is fantastic," he says, smiling as he recognizes the climbing harness. "Did Granddad help?"

I nod. "You should see it when it's on. The wings work and everything."

"Like a real swan?" He shakes his head in amazement, just like Granddad did.

I almost tell him how Granddad walked into the hospital with me this morning, how he nearly came to visit. But I don't want Dad to be disappointed when I say he didn't stay. Instead, I help him to stretch one of the wings fully so that it lies flat across his bed. He touches the primary flight feathers, the longest ones at the tip.

"What would it feel like to have wings, eh?" he murmurs. "To be up there with the swans!"

He looks out at the pale sky, and his eyes glisten. I think of my dream of Dad flying up into the sky, away, with the swans singing all around him. I think of the swans hovering above when he fell down in that field. It makes my throat tight.

He reaches across for my hand. "Don't worry," he says. "Soon I'll be waking up with a pig in my heart and a smile on my face. It'll all be fine."

I try to smile back, try to believe what he says. But it's hard when he's got tubes coming out of his arm and I can hear the nurse behind me telling Mum that his blood pressure has got higher.

I lean across and rest my head on his chest. I can still hear it, his heartbeat.

"I'll see you tomorrow," I whisper. "After the operation."

And he grasps me tightly around my shoulder. "I'll be here."

I don't want to go home. Tomorrow, first thing, they'll put Dad into a special ward to prepare for the operation, and I don't know when I'll be allowed to see him.

As Mum drives back, I bury my fingers into the swan feathers and scan the sky for birds. When we pass Saskia's old street, I notice that the *For Sale* sign has been taken down and I feel guilty for a moment that I haven't returned the calls she's left on my phone recently.

We're waiting at the traffic light near the corner restaurant when Mum asks me about Granddad, so I tell her what happened in the hospital. Mum sighs. After we pull into our driveway, she leans across to tuck a strand of hair behind my ear.

"You know why he's like that, don't you?" Mum says. "Ever since Nan died, he's had a thing about hospitals. He seems to think they make people sicker, not better."

I feel suddenly cold as I think of Dad by himself in the ward, waiting for his operation.

"But Dad will be OK, won't he?" I ask.

Mum looks over at me as she turns off the engine. "What happened to Nan won't happen to Dad."

She waits in the car. I find Jack in his room, staring straight ahead at his World Cup South Africa poster.

"Mum will drive you in now," I say.

His eyes linger on my flying model as he gets up from his desk. "I bet Dad really loved that," he says quietly.

He brushes past me and stomps down the stairs and I stare after him, surprised that he's said something nice to me for a change.

$\mathcal{L}$ater, the three of us sit in the living room with the TV on. None of us are watching it. Mum keeps getting her cell phone out of her bag to check it and Jack's bouncing his soccer ball on his knee.

"Back in an hour or so," he tells Mum, leaping up from the couch.

Mum nods but doesn't seem to register what he's said. He slams the front door behind him. Through the window, I watch him turn right toward the park. I check my watch. It's nineteen hours until Dad's operation starts. I look over at Mum.

"I'm going out, too."

I feel bad about leaving her on her own, but I can't stay in the house. It's too hot and stuffy inside, and I feel so tense. I want to run. I really want to be back at the lake, but playing soccer with Jack will have to do.

Jack's so caught up in his own thoughts that he doesn't notice me trailing him. In a moment I'll catch up and ask if he wants to kick the ball around. He jogs through the park gates, heading toward the swings. I'm about to call out to him when I see there's a girl there, kicking at the woodchips. It's Jess, the girl who tried talking to me before. Jack runs right up to her and kisses her on the mouth.

I kind of freeze for a second, watching them. It's so odd seeing Jack do that. I mean, he doesn't talk about girls or anything and he's never said he has a girlfriend. I stay where I am, just inside the park gates. I don't want to move in case Jack hears me. He would be so angry if he knew I was here. I watch Jess's hands pressing on Jack's back, grabbing at his shoulders. It makes me wonder what it feels like, being kissed like that . . . kissing. All that passion being thrown at you by another person.

I force myself to look away, and edge around the corner of the playground. I don't want to go home yet, don't want to sit with Mum and worry about Dad. I keep my head down until I get to the soccer fields. I start to run.

I lengthen my stride past the closed-up pool. Without the swan beside me, it's not as easy to go fast. I focus on the ground beneath my feet, at the blur of green grass. I crouch forward and try to imagine what it might be like to run with the wing harness around me.

I run in a big circle around the park and soon I'm back

where I began. I arch my spine and let myself breathe. The clouds all look like wings today: big, puffy, light gray wings. As I walk back to the gates, I notice there's a crowd of people in the playground now, sitting on top of the kiddie castle in a huddle. Jack's there, and Rav, and some girls. Crowy's there, too. I feel myself blush when I see him, and then feel stupid immediately. I run my arm across my face and wipe off the sweat. Even with a hood covering up Crowy's hair, he's gorgeous.

I intend to walk past before any of them can spot me, but Jack calls out.

"What are you doing here?"

"Just running."

I study his face. He doesn't look mad, maybe he hasn't clocked the fact that I must have seen him when I walked in. Or maybe he doesn't care. He's got his arm around Jess now and he's grinning. I want to scream at him until he stops looking so relaxed and happy. It doesn't seem fair somehow when Dad's so sick. I kick a piece of woodchip against the climbing wall.

"When will you be home?" I ask. "It'll be dark soon; you know Mum will worry."

He frowns and I think he's going to say something nasty, but I stare him down. He nods once, then turns to say something to Jess. Crowy crawls along the castle toward me.

"We saw you running," he calls down. "You're pretty fast."

My cheeks get even hotter. He laughs as he notices.

"You should come play soccer more often," he says.

Jack leans over and thumps him on the arm. And Crowy laughs and crawls back toward a girl I don't recognize. Jack slides down the fireman's pole and steps toward me.

"Happy now?" he grunts. He turns to say good-bye to his friends and I start walking past the swings.

"Good luck with your dad," Jess calls out.

"Thanks." Jack's voice is soft and high-pitched and doesn't sound like him at all. When he catches up with me, his mouth is clenched shut. It's as if he's fighting some emotion inside him, something he doesn't want to come out. He lopes ahead of me, heading for home.

*I*t feels like I hardly sleep. I keep dreaming about swans. I dream that Dad is flying with them, his arms held out like short, sick wings.

In the morning I pad down to Mum and Dad's bedroom. Mum's still sleeping, all alone in their huge bed. She wakes up when I crawl in next to her.

"I don't want to go to school today," I say. "I won't concentrate with Dad's operation."

Mum sighs really deeply and hugs me to her. "This is the last time," she says.

I go down to the kitchen and make toast. Jack comes in. He sits at the kitchen table and stares out the window.

"Robin," he says. "On Dad's bird feeder."

I step toward the window to see, and it doesn't fly away. Then a small, round nuthatch arrives and starts taking the seeds, too. I stand right up close to the glass. The nut-hatch looks at me with its tiny dark eyes before turning back to the seed. This makes me wonder. Maybe it's me. Maybe I've got some sort of power over birds and they all act funny around me. I place my fingers on the windowsill and stare at the nuthatch. I wait for it to stare back at me, like the swan does. I lean forward until my nose is against the glass.

"You'll scare them," Jack says.

I ignore him and focus on the birds. I start to lose feeling in the tip of my nose as I watch. The birds just keep peck-ing at the niger seeds. The robin doesn't even look at me, not once. I rest my forehead onto the glass, giving up. The birds fly away.

"See, I told you." Jack scrapes his chair from the table and starts making his breakfast.

Three hours until Dad's operation.

Then two.

The time passes so slowly. I can't concentrate on home-work, can't even concentrate on writing up the report for my flying model. In the end I sit close to Mum on the couch and we watch really awful daytime TV. My eyes keep flicking to the photograph hanging on the wall of the four of us last Christmas. Dad's got a Santa hat on and it looks like he may have had one eggnog too many. We all look so happy. When the third talk show comes on, I begin to wish I'd gone to school after all. The only excitement is when Harry texts me to tell me he's been researching how swans use their wings.

I've got it! I've found something that says exactly what swans do. Now can I come to the lake? ;-)

It's after lunchtime when we get the call. Mum takes awhile before she comes back into the living room and she looks so much more tired when she does.

"Dad's operation has been extended," she says. "The surgeons are having some problems replacing the valve. They'll let us know when they have more information."

"Let's go and wait at Granddad's," I say. "We'll be closer, then, if anything—"

Mum stops my words with a nod. "We'll get Jack on the way. School's almost over for the day, anyway."

Mum tells me to bring homework, so I take the flying model and the bits of the report I've written. I sit in the back and hug the wings to me like a kind of teddy bear. Jack's waiting outside the school gates, his phone in his hand.

My stomach churns as we make our way across town and onto the highway. I wind down my window, just a little bit, and cold air hisses onto my face. Mum pulls into Granddad's lane, the car skidding as it goes through a puddle. Jack grabs his schoolbag and I take the flying model, and we go into the house.

Granddad makes coffee. This time all of us sit on the couch and watch crappy TV. Jack pulls out his phone and starts texting. I grab mine, too, and text Harry, but only get as far as:

Dad's still in the operating room.

I don't know what to say after that. I save it while I think. Mum keeps her phone on the edge of the couch. It rings about an hour later. Granddad turns the TV down immediately and we all listen to her conversation. She sighs as she hangs up.

"They've got the valve in," she tells us. "But they're going to monitor it pretty closely over the next few hours. They want me to come in."

I wrap my arms around her waist. "I want to come with you," I say. "I want to see Dad."

Mum touches my hair. "No one else is allowed in yet, just me. I'll call when there's more news."

So Mum goes to the hospital.

Jack goes up to the spare room so he can talk on his phone without me and Granddad eavesdropping. I sit on the stairs and listen anyway, but he doesn't say anything interesting . . .

just lots of "yeah's" and "sure's" and "I'll call you tomorrow."
I bet he's talking to Jess.

I go back and sit with Granddad as he watches the news.
Unemployment has risen and the bird flu has spread to
Russia now. Granddad stares at the screen, but it doesn't
look like he's taking it in. I wonder if he feels bad now about
not staying in the hospital to see Dad. I take out my sketchbook and draw my swan. Above her, I draw more swans
arriving. Her flock. Dad has a theory about how the flock
arrives every year. He thinks they feel a kind of pull toward
their destination, as if they have a magnet inside leading
them on. Each whooper has a huge heart, too, Dad says;
they need it to keep them flying for such a huge migration.

I wish Dad's heart was as powerful.

I put my pencil down. I don't want to think about hearts.
I go to the barn instead and pick through all of Granddad's
old things. I find the bikes that I saw last time. I wheel one
out. It's old and creaky and there are cobwebs between
the spokes, but it works. Even the tires aren't that flat. I
try to cycle around the barn, which is hard because there
are boxes and tables and odds and ends all over the place.
I swerve past the operating table and see that the body of
the stuffed swan isn't there anymore. Granddad must have
moved it.

Mum calls later, but she still hasn't been able to see Dad.

"There's been another problem," she says. Her voice is

quiet and distant, as if she is speaking from another country. "Dad's had to go back on the heart machine. They have to try the whole support process again."

"Can we come in and wait with you?" I ask.

"There's no point. Even when Dad's operation is finished, they'll keep him asleep for hours. They won't let you in, and you'll only get bored."

I think of Harry waiting in his hospital room. I think of the swan on the lake. "No, I won't."

Mum doesn't let me anyway. "Go to sleep and I'll call in the morning. It'll be fine, don't worry."

But I can't sleep. There's no way I can sleep now. I just want to run all the way to the hospital and breathe air into Dad's lungs.

"This time the spare bed's mine," Jack says.

Granddad stares after him, unsure whether to get angry. "Want my bed?" he asks.

I shake my head. I'm just going to lie awake and think about Dad anyway. Granddad switches off the downstairs lights. I stare into the darkness. The couch arm smells a bit like tomato soup and there's a spring digging into my shoulder blade.

I turn over so I can see my flying model on the kitchen table. Moonlight is coming through the window and falling on the feathers. It makes them look luminous, like the wings in the Hans Christian Andersen pictures.

Eventually, Jack and Granddad stop creaking around upstairs. I listen to the muffled gushing of the toilet being flushed, the clunk of the heating going off. I wait until everything is silent, then I take out my phone again. I go back to the saved message to Harry and add to it.

Dad's still in the operating room and I can't sleep.
I just want to be in the hospital. Are you awake?

I press SEND. My phone starts ringing a few seconds later. I answer it to stop the noise. I get tingly butterfly feelings as I hear his voice.

"Come here, then," Harry says.

For a second I'm not sure that I've heard him right. "What do you mean?"

"Come to the hospital. Come here and see me."

I move from the couch into the kitchen and shut the door. "You're nuts."

"No one will know; I'll give you the door code so you can get in. Come and see me, then wait here for your dad. You'll be able to see him quicker this way, as soon as he wakes up."

His voice is whispery and soft and I wonder for a moment whether he's sleep-talking.

"I can't get to the hospital now, it's dark!"

"I thought you said your granddad's was only a couple of miles down the road?"

"It is. But it's still a couple of miles, and it's freezing. And, in case you hadn't noticed, I'm not old enough to drive."

An image of the bikes in the barn flashes into my mind but immediately I push it out. It's crazy to even think about using one of them. I pick up a pen from the table and click the end in and out. "Mum would kill me if I left Granddad's now."

There's a pause as Harry takes a sip of something. "But I'm so *bored*." He sighs his frustration. "At least talk to me, then. Tell me about your dad. What happened?"

I look out the window at the blackness beyond. I keep playing with the pen as I tell Harry about waiting with Mum and getting the phone calls and about Mum rushing off.

"I hate waiting here," I say. "I just want to do something."

"What's it like?" he says. "At your granddad's?"

"Messy. His couch smells like tomato soup."

I tell him about the hundreds of stars I can see from Granddad's kitchen window, ones that I can't usually see from my bedroom at home.

"I can see stars through my window, too," he says quietly. I shut my eyes for a moment and it feels like he's in the room with me.

"What else can you see?" I ask.

"There's a big moon, and a silver lake." He pauses again. "I can see the swan, too, the moonlight's right on her."

I think about what it might be like to be in Harry's room at night, sitting with him and looking at the swan.

"Is she OK?"

I can hear Harry shift in his bed to look. "Should I go down there and find out?"

"To the lake?"

"Where else?"

I can hear the smile in Harry's voice. Again, there's that tingly feeling in my stomach.

"You're not going to go down there alone," I whisper.

"I might. I might if you don't come to the hospital really soon and go there with me."

He laughs a little. Waits for me to speak. I swallow slowly, but I'm all out of answers.

"It'll be cold down there," I say. "It's too crazy."

"I don't care."

"I thought you were scared of outside places."

"I'm not scared," he says, indignant now.

I think of the swan floating by herself. I imagine walking with Harry, through the trees, to get to her. I think of finding Dad afterward, at first light. Then I think of the alternative: sitting in this cold kitchen, waiting for the morning, and worrying. I listen to Harry breathing.

"Promise you won't die on me?" I say.

"Promise."

And, like that, I agree.

*I*mmediately I regret what I've said and I try to call him back. But Harry doesn't answer. He sends me one text message.

See you soon! :-) The number for the door is 12023.

Harry is too sick for a midnight trip to the lake, I know this, and I'd get in so much trouble if anyone caught us. Besides, what would Granddad do if he woke up and found I'd gone? I lean my head onto my flying model. The feathers smell dusty and old, nothing like the damp, fishy smell of the wings of the swan on the lake. I wonder about her, floating alone, with no other flock members to huddle up to. Do swans get lonely? Cold? Dad's said before that, without their flock, a bird's chance of survival isn't very good. And Harry said maybe she'd fly if she found her flock. But the problem is she needs to fly in the first place to be able to find them.

I look back out at the star-filled sky. Dad's alone, too, in his hospital room, needing support from a machine. But he's not the only one alone.

I text Harry one more time.

We are going to get in so much trouble. I'll be there in 20 mins.

I leave a note for Granddad on the kitchen table. Then I carry the flying model through the hall. I take my coat from the hooks beside the front door. There's a faded green hat hanging underneath it, one of Granddad's, so I take that, too. I go out the back way, pushing the door handle really, really slowly. I shut it behind me with a small clunk. I look up, check that the light in Granddad's room hasn't gone on. This is stupid, what I'm doing, but my feet lead me to the barn anyway.

The wind sends leaves spinning past my face. When a big gust makes the metal sides of the barn creak, I draw back the rusty bolt. I find the bike I was riding earlier and wheel it out. The handlebars feel like solid rods of ice. I try tying the wings to the bike. They're too big to balance across the handlebars, and I can't find anywhere else to put them. I have to wear them.

I thread my legs into the harness and tighten the buckles across my chest and stomach. I leave my arms free to steer the bike, and leave the wings folded in on my back. My teeth are already chattering as I wheel the bike around the side of the house, and I'm glad of the extra weight and warmth of the wings.

I set off, the bike wobbling a bit on the uneven ground of Granddad's lane. I pedal into blackness. The bike skids on ice as I take a left onto the main road and I almost end up in the gutter, but somehow I manage to keep upright. I move toward the center of the road, where the pavement looks dryer. I pedal faster. There are no cars, no people. It's too cold. I pass the strip of shops where the Indian takeout place is, and then it's just a long, straight road to the hospital. There's one hill to go up; after that it'll be downhill all the way.

I stand on the pedals as I get to the hill, using my body weight to push down. I watch the pavement move beneath me. Fast at first, then slower and slower as I near the top. The muscles in my legs start to quiver, but at least I'm not cold anymore. I grip the handlebars tightly and force myself to keep going. I feel my heart thudding in my chest. I hope Dad's heart is beating just as strongly.

Then, finally, I'm there. At the brow of the hill. I stop pedaling and put my feet on the road. The lights of the town spread out behind me. Granddad's house is somewhere in the darkness between me and them. I look ahead at the large block of lights that make up the hospital. There's a space behind the hospital that looks darker than anywhere. The lake. Somewhere, in the middle of all that blackness, floats the swan. Does she know I'm coming?

I feel the wind behind me, making my coat flap. I angle the bike to face down the hill. Before I push off, I have a crazy idea. I unfold the wings, stretch them out across my back. They bounce with the wind, their feathers fluttering around my ears. The bike is inching forward already.

I let go of the brakes. The wind shoves me hard and pushes me down the hill. I grip the handlebars, trying to keep them steady. The wings work like a sail and I go faster and faster toward the hospital. I go so fast that the bike starts to shake. I'm too scared to touch the brakes now. A slip left and I'll be veering into the trees at the edge of the road. A slip right and I'll be in the other lane. My wings begin to make a low throbbing sound. I must be going faster than a car. I feel faster than anything. It's like I'm flying. If I had the guts to angle my wings properly, to make them shift and catch the wind, I'm sure I could take off.

I wheel the bike through the parking lot and lock it to a rack near the entrance. I see Mum's car and wonder where she is in the hospital. Harry's told me that there are family bedrooms on the fifth floor where his mum sleeps sometimes, and I wonder whether Mum has been allowed to sleep there. Or maybe she's dozing in the uncomfortable chair again. I feel a pang of guilt, wonder whether it's her I should be trying to find in this hospital instead of Harry.

I take an empty elevator to the third floor. My footsteps echo in the corridors. At the door to Harry's ward, I stop to peer inside. There are no nurses at the desk, so I take a breath and quickly key in the numbers Harry texted me. The door clicks open. I try not to make a sound as I walk past rooms of sleeping kids. Every part of me is listening for noises, waiting for a nurse to stop me.

Harry is sitting up in bed, waiting. There's a laptop and sheets of paper spread out over his blankets. I close the door behind me.

"Why didn't you answer when I called you back?" I whisper.

He smiles slowly. "You wouldn't have come in then."

"This is crazy," I say. I walk around his bed and crouch near the window. This way, if a nurse comes in, they might not be able to see me right away. I place the wings on the bottom of his bed. "If we get caught we'll be in so much trouble."

"We won't get caught." Harry sweeps his hair back from his forehead, sending a few more loosened strands floating down. It's thinning badly now. I look away from it quickly as he sees me watching.

"Trust me," he continues. "I know exactly when the nurses change shifts and when they come to check on me. It's the same every night. They've just been, and they won't come again for at least another five hours."

I'm not sure I believe him, he could just be saying it to let me think it's OK. I feel sick as I think about all the things that could happen to Harry when we're out there alone.

"I'm not sure this is a good idea."

Harry's hand moves across his blankets until his fingers rest on the back of mine. I look down at them. They feel so light and cold against my skin. I almost turn my hand over and hold them right. I would, I think, if I wasn't so worried.

"Hey," he says quietly. "What if this is the only time we can ever do this?"

"It won't be. After your transplant and after Dad's better, we can do whatever you want."

His fingers press more firmly against my skin. "Maybe," he says. "But what if I don't survive it?"

"What?" My voice seems to echo around his room, far too loud.

"Fifty percent chance," he says, shrugging slightly.

"You never told me that." I keep staring at him. I know this transplant thing is serious, but I didn't realize quite how serious. My stomach sinks. First Dad, and now Harry. Both of them so sick. Both of them could die.

"Why would I tell you?" I feel his fingers tracing patterns on my skin. "As soon as you say something like that, people back away."

"I wouldn't."

He takes his fingers off my hand as he closes down his laptop. This time it's my skin that feels cold.

"Why only fifty percent?" I say quietly.

He gathers up the papers on his bed. "The problem is they have to find exactly the right match for a bone marrow transplant," he explains. "And even then my body might not like it. It might shut down when they try to stick this other person's bone marrow in me, might give up."

There's something so calm about his expression. It's almost as if what he's saying doesn't bother him. But it has to. He might die. How can anyone be calm about that? I run my eyes across his cheeks and forehead. He doesn't look sick. At least not if I don't look at his hair. He looks like any other boy I might be sitting in a hospital room with at half past midnight. Only he isn't any other boy. With his wide smile and bright eyes, he really is beautiful. I breathe in quickly as it hits me. He's more beautiful even than Crowy.

Harry grins quickly. He's got his answer. "I knew you'd come with me." He pulls back his blankets and swings his legs out.

I just stare up at him. How can he be so sick when he's just leaped out of bed? I study him, looking for clues. His pajamas have small pictures of sailing ships on them. He sticks a sweater over the top when he sees me looking.

"My mum's got no taste," he says.

I stand, then sit back down on the bed, then stand again. I'm crazy nervous.

"What if you get sick?" I whisper. "By the lake. I wouldn't know what to do."

"I won't. Anyway . . ." He grabs his cell phone from the bedside table. ". . . that's what these are for. All the useful numbers are stored in it."

He digs around in the closet near the door, pulls out a

black duffel coat and a scarf. I take out the hat I took from Granddad's and hand it over to him.

"You'd better wear this as well," I say. "It's cold out there."

He touches my arm. "Thanks, Isla."

I freeze, wait for him to say more. He's close to me, close enough to hug. But he just turns back to the closet and takes out a pair of sneakers. He sits down on the bed to put them on.

"I've found out loads about how swans use their wings," he says. "You don't need to worry when we get down there; I'll tell you what to do."

"I'm still not sure I can run with these things on, you know."

"Doesn't matter. We'll go down to the lake, I'll see the swan, you give the wings a go, and if it works, it works. If it doesn't . . ."

"I'm glad you think it's a mad idea, too," I say quickly. I reach to grab a folded woolen blanket from the shelf in the closet and force it into his arms.

"Now we just need the wheelchair from the next room," he says.

"Wheelchair?"

"If you want to be certain of nothing happening . . . I'm not sure I can walk the whole way."

I sneak back into the corridor, open the next door down. It's a kind of storeroom. I grab the wheelchair and wheel it back to Harry. He gets in and I place the blanket over his lap, then tuck it around his legs, nice and tight.

"If anyone asks, we're just going for a wheel around the wards, OK?"

I nod. "I'll say you can't sleep."

He starts wheeling toward the door, but I'm suddenly too nervous to follow him.

"Come on, then, Bird Girl," he whispers. "Let's go."

He looks back, his face serious, and I can see there's no way he's going to back down now. He's going to the lake whether I am or not. I should be glad about it. The lake will be different at night, darker and quieter, and he'll get to see the swan. It's what I wanted after all, isn't it?

"It's your fault if you get sick," I say.

Harry holds his hand against his chest, looks at me solemnly. "I take full responsibility." He gives me a small grin. I want to catch it and keep it.

I stretch Granddad's hat farther down over Harry's head. Strands of his hair fall in my hands. He watches my reaction.

"I'm going to shave it soon," he says. "I'm starting to look like a patchy rabbit." He sighs suddenly and the grin disappears.

I crouch down so my head is level with his. "No, you don't," I say. "You look like a baby bird who hasn't grown all its feathers yet."

He muffles a laugh. "Trust you to think of that."

I tuck his scarf into his sweater, zip his coat all the way up to his chin, and pull the blanket tighter around him. "Don't get me into trouble tonight," I say.

He rolls his eyes at me, but he lets me tuck. I grab the wings from the bed and place them on his lap.

52

It's a miracle that we get out of the hospital without any-one stopping us. I wheel Harry along the edge of the parking lot, my head darting from side to side every few seconds.

"Stop it!" Harry hisses. "You'll make us look suspicious."

I almost laugh. "Yeah, like we don't already, wheeling around a freezing parking lot at nearly one in the morning?"

My heart is thudding. It feels as though it's beating even faster than when I was on the bike. And the butterflies are back, bashing at my ribs every time I look at Harry. I stop near the sagging shed and hold my hand to my chest. What if I collapse like Dad did? What if my heart's stuffed up, too?

"Can you hear that?" I ask Harry, still with my hand on my chest. "My heart sounds too loud."

But Harry's more interested in pulling back the fence

wire. "Stop panicking and just get me through this thing," he says.

He moves the wheelchair right up against the fence so he can get a grip. I help him, opening the gap wide enough for his wheelchair to fit through.

"I hope this thing's got four-wheel drive," I say.

I wheel him over the pile of beer cans and cigarette butts, and see Harry grit his teeth as the chair jolts. I'm glad for the clear sky and moonlight. It gives me a chance to scan the trees, checking for shadows. My heartbeat slows as we get farther in, and I start to relax.

We get to the lake. Harry holds the wings tightly on his lap as he takes it all in. He pulls his phone out of his pocket and checks that he has reception, then drags his scarf up to his chin.

"Where is she?" he whispers.

"She'll come."

As soon as I say it, I see her. She floats across the dark water like a ghost. The moonlight's bouncing off her feathers, making them glow. I wonder if her white adult feathers are starting to come through. I wheel Harry toward the bank, pushing harder as the tires churn up the soft ground. The swan keeps swimming until she's right in front of us. She stares first at me and then at Harry. There's no fear in her eyes. I wait for Harry to see that and be scared of her. But all he says is, "I don't have any bread."

The swan stops looking at him. She inches onto the bank and waddles over to me, gurgling softly as she places her beak against my leg. There's that familiar rush of cold zipping right through my body. I glance over at Harry.

"You see?" I say. "She's not normal."

Harry grins. "She's great. Show her your flying model."

I take it from where it lies folded on Harry's lap and open the wings so she can see it all. She stretches her neck forward and runs her beak over the feathers. She hisses suddenly as she gets it caught in a loop of Velcro and I help her untangle herself. I'm wondering if she thinks it's weird that I'm showing her wings. Maybe it's like someone showing me two human legs.

"Harry's got this crazy idea," I tell her. "He thinks we can use my project to help you fly."

She tips her head to the side when she hears my voice, and Harry laughs.

"She's listening," he says. "Just like a dog."

I watch her blink quickly as she turns her head to the sound of his voice. "Do you think she can understand us?" I say.

Harry laughs again. "Maybe." He shrugs. "Are you sure she's not someone's pet?"

I shake my head. "I saw her, that day when the swans crashed into the wires; I'm sure it was her."

He watches her carefully. Now that he doesn't have the

wings to hold, his hands are clasped tightly in his lap.

"You can touch her, you know. She lets me."

I reach forward to the swan to show him, run the back of my fingers down her neck. I like the way she murmurs softly in her throat as I do. But Harry leans back in his chair, away from her.

"Are you scared?" I ask, laughing. "She doesn't bite."

"Maybe she just doesn't bite *you*."

I look back at the swan, find her deep dark eyes and really stare into them.

"How about it, then, bird?" I say. "Will you fly this time?"

We go to the other side of the lake. The track is wider here and the hospital lights farther away. The wind is stronger, too, much stronger. It whips against us, making Harry hunker down into the blankets. The swan follows us, keeping pace on the water.

She stops for a moment, turning her beak to the wind and smelling it. The wind grabs at her feathers. It's icy, as if it's coming from a faraway place, and it's pulling us away from here, dragging us somewhere else.

I jump up and down to get warm, then pull the blankets tighter around Harry.

"You OK?" I ask. "Not too cold?"

He shakes his head impatiently. "Put your wings on," he says. "Show her what you're going to do." He's smiling as he says it, but I can see his skin looks grayer and colder.

"Fine, but we're not staying much longer," I say.

As I thread my legs through the harness the swan swims right up close, curious about what I'm doing. I ask Harry to help me fasten the Velcro strips and tighten the buckles across my chest. He smiles. His fingers are already on the loops, bluish and stiff. I breathe warm air onto them.

He glances up at me, his eyes like beacons. "This is it," he whispers. "Good luck, Isla."

"It's her you should be saying that to," I tell him. "She's the one flying."

Harry tells me what he's learned about how swans take off. He explains how a swan angles its feathers to the wind as it runs across the water. He gets me to practice by turning my primary flight feathers so that the wind pushes behind them. The swan beats her own wings, watching me. I just hope she understands.

"Is she ready?" Harry asks, looking at the swan.

"Only one way to find out."

I look down the runway of the lakeside track. I bend my arms and pull the wires one by one, testing them.

"Just listen to what I'm telling you to do," Harry says. "I'll shout instructions."

"I'll try."

The swan holds her black-eyed gaze in mine.

"You ready, swan?"

Her hiss makes me shiver. It almost sounds like a "yes."

She opens her beak wide, begins to honk and whoop. She moves her head up and down in time with the sounds she's making, beats her wings. I laugh suddenly.

"What's she doing?" Harry asks.

"It's what whooper swans do before they fly," I explain. "It's kind of like a ritual, head bobbing and honking; the whole flock does it."

Harry raises his eyebrows. "Maybe you should do it, too?"

"I'm not doing that!"

Her noises increase to a trumpeting sound until she rises and beats her wings against the water's surface. I can almost feel her excitement, her urge to fly.

"Now," Harry says. "Go now."

I start to run. I put my head down and tuck the wings behind me, exactly like Harry's explained. I concentrate on running straight. It's really hard because the wings keep pulling me from side to side with each stride I take. The wind is pushing from behind, pushing me faster. The swan rises on the water, still honking. I have a strange urge to shout as well. It's only because Harry's there that I don't. I try to pick up speed, but the wings feel so heavy on my shoulders. The swan keeps one eye on me the whole time. She's watching everything.

I can hear Harry, shouting above the wind, telling me what to do. I angle my arms and separate the primary flight feathers. I try to turn them. The swan copies every movement. It's amazing. It's as if she understands we're trying to help her.

"Now beat your wings," Harry yells.

I don't intend to beat them so slowly, but it's seriously difficult with the wind and the running and everything else. It feels like I'm using every single muscle to bring the wings to the ground and back up again. The swan keeps pace with me easily. I spring up onto my toes, try to run faster.

A gust of wind pushes against my wings. It shoves me so hard that my feet lift from the ground. Just for a moment. Then they touch the track again. I keep running. The swan is going to lift off any second, I just know it. The wind forces me upward, lifts me again. Drops me down. I wait for the swan to take off. She's still watching me. I turn my wrists until the feathers angle into the wind again. I push myself to take bigger strides. I'm running faster than ever before. The swan's feet are hardly touching the water now. She's almost there. I can feel it.

Then something inside my chest seems to twist and flap. It feels like my heart's about to explode. Maybe I'm going to collapse, just like Dad did. But I don't slow down, I can't. Not until she takes off.

"Go on!" I plead.

There's another twinge inside me. I bring my wings inward, grappling for my chest. The swan brings her wings in, too. My heart is beating so fast and so loud, it's like it has wings of its own and is trying to escape through my ribs. But the swan is nodding at me. She's taking off!

Then a huge gust of wind shoves me sideways. Forward. Upward. I feel it rushing all around, over my body and through my wings. It turns me cold. Pulls at me. Sucks me up, up . . . I try to struggle against it, but it's no use. The ground peels away from my feet like a Band-Aid. I straighten my wings to steady myself. Try to find the ground again. My feet are floating; there's air underneath them! I stretch my toes down to feel the path again, but I can't. I can't do anything apart from move my arms up and down. Keep beating. Keep beating or I'll fall. I gasp as I realize what I'm doing.

I'm flying!

At least it feels like it. I breathe in huge, frozen mouthfuls of air. The ground is farther away now. This can't be possible. I'm not doing this. I can't be.

Out of the corner of my eye I see the swan. She's beside me. Her wings are making a slight whistling sound and her neck is straight. For a second I can't do anything but watch her. The wind is sliding off her wings and sweeping over my own. She looks at me, opens her beak into a screaming call. I shout, too, my voice whipping backward with the wind. She's done it.

I stop beating my wings to watch her, hoping I'll glide

softly to the ground. But suddenly a gust of wind pushes me over the water. I look back, try to find Harry on the bank. Call out to him. I scrabble through the air, try to get back to the track, but it's no use. I start to tip. Start to fall. Down toward the lake.

I land flat on my back in the reeds near the bank. My wings stretch across the vegetation, holding me up from the water. I don't move. I don't want to sink. The stars above me are trembling, and my body is swaying with the reeds.

I turn my head so I can see the bank. Harry's left his wheelchair and he's coming toward me. He's calling out, but I can't understand what he's saying. My ears feel full of water, and everything is blurry. I want to shut my eyes and sink down, down, into the reeds. My feet slip, and my shoes begin to fill. The water is so cold.

There's a splashing sound as Harry gets into the lake.

"What are you doing?" I try to say. "You'll get wet."

He's knee-deep already. I turn around, which makes me sink farther and my legs go under. I gasp. The water's like ice. I try to find a foothold but it's too muddy. My sneakers get stuck. Harry reaches me, presses close to undo the

Velcro strips around my arms. Then he starts dragging me by the wings. He's stronger than he looks. Reeds slap me in the face and my wings get tangled in everything. I force my feet into the mud, force myself to stand. Grabbing at Harry, I try to steady myself. He's laughing.

"That was amazing," he says. "How did you do that?"

I keep my eyes on him, try to focus. "She flew, didn't she?"

"I saw her." A smile spreads out slowly over Harry's face. "You did, too. At least, you were about three feet above the ground."

"How . . . ?"

He shrugs. "The wind?"

His teeth are chattering, but I don't think he's noticed. I don't think he's even aware that he's in the water. I yank my arms away from the wings and touch his chin.

"Your lips are blue," I say.

He stops and reaches up to where my hands are. He puts his hands on top of mine. He feels warm. I wasn't expecting that.

"You did it," he says. "Your swan flew."

He looks so happy. It makes me smile. I wonder where she's headed now. A part of me is sad she's gone, but . . .

"Dad will be pleased," I murmur.

There are polka dots jumping in front of my eyes and Harry's face is rippling like the lake. I'm standing so close to him, close enough to feel his warm breath on the end of my nose. His eyes skim over the drooping wings on my back. He reaches toward me and brushes his fingers against my cheek.

"Bird Girl," he says softly.

His fingertips feel light as feathers. My skin tingles where they touch. I try to steady myself, grabbing him around the neck. His skin is soft, but he doesn't feel fragile. He's solid. Real. His breath falters as it hits my cheek. He's so close. His smile is blurring. He leans forward. I can feel my heart racing and fluttering again. I feel his breath against my lips. I shut my eyes.

Then he does it: He kisses me. He's so soft and gentle. His lips are trembling, almost breakable. But they're warm, and they're moving against mine.

He pulls back, smiles a little. His breath comes in a rush.

"Sorry, I . . ."

Even from this close up, I can see that he's blushing. It's lovely, seeing that color in his cheeks.

"It's OK," I whisper.

I want him to kiss me again, but instead I start smiling, which makes him smile, and then we laugh. It makes me breathless. And it makes his face swirl. Everything feels good now. The swan flew; Harry kissed me. Maybe it's a sign that things are getting better.

55

*A*fter a moment, I step away from him.

"Where did she fly?" I ask. "What direction?"

"Not far." Harry nods at the lake behind me. "When you fell, she landed."

"Landed?"

"But she flew a whole loop before that."

I shake my head, confused. "Why didn't she just keep flying?"

I want to say more, but I can't get the words out. Instead, I see the lake getting closer, the reeds spinning past my head. Suddenly, Harry's hands are grabbing at my shoulders.

"You need to get out of here," he says.

He pushes me toward the bank. My wings drag behind me, snapping off bits of reed and taking them along. I crawl out of the water. I lie back on the track and look across at the trees.

"Did I just imagine that?"

Harry sticks his head over me, his face upside down. "No way."

His fingers dart over the harness, loosening the buckles, drawing the wings away. I can breathe. I turn over onto my knees, coughing. It feels as if I've swallowed the whole lake. I look back at the water and try to search for the swan, but it's too dark to see anything. All I can make out is the flattened reed bed where I landed. Harry's got his hand on my back, but his face is blurry again. Suddenly, I know I'm going to be sick. I throw up brown water, bits of reed. It puddles around me, seeps into the dirt. Slowly my eyes begin to focus.

Harry drags the wings away. I look at the slight smile on his face, thinking how perfect it looks, remembering how it felt to have it close to mine. I remember the feeling as my feet left the track, too. The fluttering in my chest.

Harry puts his arm around my shoulder and leans us back against the wheelchair. I can feel him breathing, heavier now. He rests his cheek against my hair.

"We better get you back to the hospital," I say.

We find the swan on the other side, near the place where she always waits for me. I stop pushing the wheelchair when I see her, and she floats toward us. I look at her carefully, searching for clues as to why she didn't just fly away. I grip the handles of Harry's chair.

"Do you want to try again?" Harry's voice is muffled by the scarf wrapped around him.

I see how cold he is. His skin's paler than eggshells. I can almost see his veins through it. I tuck the blankets right up to his neck and the hat down over his ears. His teeth are chattering, too, and he's clasping the sodden swan wings tight to his chest.

"I have to get you back," I say. I want to touch my lips to his and make his cheeks turn pink again. "This was stupid, coming here."

Harry reaches out from under the blankets and grabs my arm. "No, it wasn't."

He looks at me, his eyes sparkling. Suddenly, I want more than anything to make him warm again. I glance at the swan, check where she is one last time, then wheel Harry back to the hospital. We go in the Emergency entrance this time, behind a woman who's about to give birth. Everyone's too bothered about her to worry about us. It's weird, being back here, wheeling Harry past the small blue waiting room that has another family in it now.

The wheelchair leaves muddy tire tracks behind us.

"I think we have to ditch it," I say. "Someone might follow them and find us. Are you all right to walk?"

Harry nods, but he doesn't look all right. The skin under his eyes looks bruised and dark and he's breathing heavily. I stick my arm around him. He smells like lake.

It's just turned two by the time we get back to his ward. I walk ahead of him down the corridor, checking for nurses. But we get into his room unnoticed. Harry sits on his bed and looks at the floor, his eyelids starting to close. I root around in his small closet until I find a pair of dry pajamas.

"Put these on," I say. "You need to get warm."

He just holds them on his lap and stares up at me. I think he's waiting for me to leave the room. But there's no time for being polite. I turn around and start putting away the blanket we'd taken. When I think I've given him enough time, I turn back. He's changed his pajama bottoms but he's struggling with the top. I go over. He's too tired to object. I can't help glancing at his chest as I pull off his pajama sleeves. There are two white tubes there. They look like wires, the sort you plug into the back of a TV, but they are coming directly out of him with see-through tape sticking them firmly to his chest. His skin is yellowish and bruised around where they come out. I guess these must be the tubes they feed his treatment through: his Hickman line.

When I look back at Harry's face, he's watching me carefully. Probably wondering if I'm freaked out. I am, but I'm not going to show it. So I just pick up the dry pajama top and chuck it at him to put on.

I turn away to the window, but I'm still thinking about those tubes. I start panicking then, really panicking. What if water from the lake has got into them? What if I've just made him really, really sick? I hear him getting into bed. I open his window and chuck his wet pajamas down into the dumpster. They land right in it.

"She shoots, she scores!"

I hear Harry's soft laugh. I turn back. His skin seems to be sagging with tiredness, his eyes so much darker. He looks so different from the way he looked at the lake only half an hour ago. He's sick again . . . sicker than I've ever seen him. Perhaps I dreamt up the boy who came with me tonight.

"Are you OK? Seriously?" I ask.

"Stop worrying."

I take a towel from the closet and wipe up the puddles on the floor. I dig back in for more of Harry's clothes.

"Take anything you want," Harry murmurs.

There's a pair of blue track pants that will be baggy on me, but at least they're not wet. I take off my jeans and slip them on instead. Again, my jeans follow the pajamas out the window and land in the dumpster. I dry the wings as best I can and place these under Harry's bed.

"Can I leave them there?" I ask. "Just while I go and see Dad?"

He nods. He reaches toward me and I thread my fingers through his. I place my other hand on top, warming them. I grin at him, stupidly, and still can't believe he kissed me. After a moment, his eyes start to close again. I sit next to him on his bed and lean back against the wall. I watch his lips, quivering a little with each breath he takes.

"Please be OK," I whisper.

I wait until I see the color come back into his cheeks. Then I shut my eyes for a moment, too, and the room starts swaying. I feel as though I'm flying.

*H*arry's there when I wake up, close beside me. His skin is warmer now, and his breath is steady. He's still got his hand in mine. I don't want to leave him, but I don't want his nurse to come in and find me here, either. Carefully, I unthread my fingers. I watch him for a moment. Did it all happen? The kiss in the lake? The flying?

I go back to the Emergency Room. I don't know why. I suppose it's one of the only places I can go where I can wait and no one wants to know why I'm there. I hug my knees to my chest and watch everyone. No one says anything to me. There's a guy about Jack's age with blood on his face, and a few other people waiting. It's started raining. I can see it pelting Granddad's bike every time the glass doors slide open. It looks like it's set in. There are no emergencies for a whole hour. I rest my head onto my knees and sleep.

When it gets to five and it's still raining, I text Mum.

Couldn't sleep so rode one of Granddad's bikes to the hospital.
Can I see Dad yet?

She calls back five minutes later.

"It's miles!" she says. "And it's on the main road."

Thankfully she doesn't say anything about the rain. Perhaps she hasn't noticed that it's been constant for the last couple of hours. I walk through the corridors to meet her in the café, which isn't open yet. She hugs me to her.

"Don't do that again," she says. "No matter how sick Dad gets. You could have got run over; anything could have happened!"

I nod, brushing away her concern. "How's Dad?"

She pulls me down onto her knee. "He's made it through," she says, quietly. "You might be able to see him in a few hours."

"The valve?"

"His body seems to have accepted it; he's off the support machine."

She rests her head on top of mine and clasps me tighter. I'm expecting her to say something about Harry's track pants, or something about how damp and muddy my top is . . . or even to get angry again because I cycled in. But she just breathes in deeply, and sighs.

"You smell like trees," she says. "Of wild things and rain."

*M*um calls Granddad to tell him I'm here. I don't know what Granddad's reaction is exactly, but it's loud. Mum holds the phone away from her ear so that even I can hear him shout. She tilts her eyes skyward as she looks at me.

"They'll come in and meet us soon," she says as she hangs up. "He was worried, Isla, you shouldn't have snuck off like that."

After the café is open and we've had breakfast, we go up to the Intensive Care Unit. A nurse meets us at the door.

"He's still under the anesthetic," she says to Mum. "Still sleeping." Her eyes scan down my clothes. "It might be best if you don't stay long."

She makes us stick these plastic bag things over our shoes, then leads us inside. The room feels different to anywhere else I've been in the hospital. It's quieter, muted somehow, and it doesn't seem to smell of anything. The only sounds are beeps and shuffles and a strange soft whirring. No one is talking; perhaps it's not allowed. Sky blue curtains surround the beds.

The nurse pushes aside one set of curtains. Dad is sleeping inside with tubes leading into his nose and arms, and a beeping monitor beside his bed. Dad's bed is a lot higher than his last one; it's up to my chest. There are no chairs to sit down on. Mum closes the curtains behind us. We're in our own little world in here: me, Mum, and Dad. A small, blue square world. I pull the curtains across a little farther, closing up the gap to the rest of the room. Then I hold Mum's hand.

Dad's lying very still and he's making a rasping sound as he breathes. It's as if he's got a cheese grater in his throat and all the air has to go through it. Mum leans across and touches his hair. Dad's eyes flicker and I think he's going to wake up. Mum's hand tightens around mine.

"Gray?" Mum tries to get his attention. "Gray, I've brought Isla for you."

When she doesn't get a response from Dad, she looks over to me. I don't think she knows what to say. She moves her other hand to Dad's, gives it a squeeze. For a moment we're all connected, the life from me running through Mum and into Dad. The silence wraps around us like the curtain.

I want to tell Dad everything. I want to tell him about my

strange night at the lake with Harry and the swan. I want to tell him that we got her to fly. I even open my mouth. But the words stay inside, too loud for this ward, and Dad closes his eyes again and the moment passes.

Mum squeezes my hand. "Let's leave him to sleep," she whispers.

She leans down to kiss Dad lightly on the forehead.

"I'll bring Jack later," she says.

I wonder if I should kiss Dad, too. I'm still a bit damp from the lake and I smell like mud. I touch the back of his hand instead. His skin is smooth and waxy, not very warm.

Jack's waiting at the ward desk.

"Granddad went ballistic," he says, glaring at me. "I've never seen him so angry. Thought he was going to crash the car or something when he drove here."

"It was only a couple of miles," I say. "I left a note."

Jack shrugs. "Couldn't you just have waited until we got up?"

A nurse looks sternly at us from behind the ward desk; we're making too much noise. Mum grabs Jack and steers him in to see Dad. The nurse goes with them. I find a seat next to the desk and lean my head back against the wall, feeling my eyes close. My body starts swaying and it feels like I'm flying again, far, far above the hospital . . . right up in the clouds. There's a flock flying with me, helping to carry me forward.

Then cold fingers are shaking me. "You're exhausted," Mum whispers. "Better get you home."

We walk through the corridors.

"I want to see Harry," I say. "I won't be long."

Mum puts her hands on her hips as if she's going to stop me.

"I'll be in the café in five minutes, I promise," I say.

Jack's walking on ahead, ignoring me completely. Mum raises her eyebrows, but I hurry past, not waiting to hear what she's going to say.

A nurse clicks open the door for me. "Harry's pretty tired."

"I just need to get something I left in there," I say. "I'll only be a second."

She lets me go, but trails behind. I half run to get ahead of her. As soon as I get in Harry's room, I take off my coat, find the wings underneath the bed, and bundle them inside it. I clasp my arms around them tightly as I stand. I look at him. His eyes are still shut, his body turned toward the window now. His mouth moves a little as he dreams. I want to stay with him until he wakes.

But the nurse comes in, looking at me warily. I step around her, not wanting her to think too much about the bundle in my arms.

"I'll come back when he's awake," I say, squeezing out the door.

I keep my head down as I go through the ward and make

it out before anyone asks any questions. I hurry back to the café.

Mum looks at the bundled-up coat in my arms. "What's that?" she says.

"Just my flying model."

I try to make my voice sound casual so she doesn't ask me anything more. She wants to, I can see in her face that she has a million questions. So I shift the model to my side, away from her, and keep walking. I get her to tell me about Dad instead.

"Well, his temperature is still up," she says. "So he's not out of the woods yet."

"I thought he'd be awake by now," Jack says.

They talk more about Dad's operation, and I traipse behind them. I unlock the bike from the rack. I have to wheel it with one hand because of the flying model, but I get it to the car.

Jack grumbles as he tries to fit the bike into the trunk. "What's up with you, anyway?" he says. "What's with all the weird things you've been doing?"

"What weird things?"

He rolls his eyes. "You sure you're all right?"

I shrug. If I told Jack about the trip to the lake and the swan following me and the wind lifting me up into the air, he'd be convinced I was going mad.

We pull up at school. Jack's out of the car immediately.

"Call me if anything changes with Dad," he says before slamming the door. He jogs in through the gates.

Mum turns around to study my face. She picks a twig from my hair.

"Think we'd better just take you home," she says.

That night, I dream I'm at the lake. Only it's Harry wearing the wing model, not me. He beats the wings firmly and regularly and runs after the swan. I watch him speed down the track, away from me. I want to go with him, but I can't. I'm sitting in his wheelchair this time and my legs won't work. His feet lift from the track. He takes off. Starts to soar into the sky. Higher and higher. He follows the swan, screeching as he goes. I lean forward in the wheelchair and watch his body getting smaller. There's an ache in my chest as I watch him. But I can't take my eyes from him. I'm scared that if I do, he'll just disappear. I'm scared I'll never see him again.

Mum's on the phone when I wake up. I sit on the top step of the stairs and listen to her end of the conversation. When she hangs up, she stands with her head pressed against the wall with her eyes shut. After a while, I go down the stairs and stand next to her. She slips her hand into mine.

"Dad's not too well," she says softly. "His temperature is still up and he has swelling."

"What does that mean?"

"They're not sure. Either his body is rejecting the valve, or . . . they think he might have an infection."

I shut my eyes for a second, too. "Like Nan had?"

Mum's fingers clasp tighter around mine. "I don't know, Isla, they won't tell me."

"Are you going to tell Granddad?"

"I don't know."

We keep standing there in the hall, just thinking. I feel

sick. Nan got so ill once she got that infection, she died so quickly.

"How did he get it?" I whisper.

I almost tell Mum about the wings, about going to the lake with Harry and falling in the water. What if it's my fault Dad's sick? What if he's sick because of the mud and bits of reed that I had on me when I visited him? But Mum just sighs deeply.

"Who knows, babe? They're doing more tests today."

I swallow slowly. "Will he be OK?"

"Of course." She nods. "It's nothing serious yet, they just thought we should know."

She drives us to school anyway.

"There's no use sitting around being worried," she says. She looks at me in the rearview mirror. "And you're not missing another day. I'll call you on your phones if he gets any worse."

I hold my flying model on my lap. It's filthy. I run my hands over the wings and try to brush off some of the dried mud. It no longer looks like the beautiful thing Granddad and I made in the barn.

At the school gates, Jack hesitates. "I'll be at the soccer field at lunchtime . . . if Mum calls."

He jogs on to meet his friends, who are waiting inside. Jess is there, too. He says something to her, then puts his arm over her shoulder as he starts to walk. He glances back at me, raises the watch on his other arm, and wiggles it in the air.

"You're late!"

No one is at the gates waiting for me. Not even Sophie, and I've told her about what's going on with Dad. Once again, I wish that Saskia was still here. There's no way she'd ever let me walk in alone. I trudge in behind Jack's friends, wishing I was part of his group. They always seem so close, such a pack. I'm jealous for a second until I see the way that Rav and Deano are looking at the wing model I'm carrying. They lean in toward each other and share some sort of joke. Then Crowy slaps the back of Deano's head.

"She's right there," he hisses.

He turns to see if I've heard whatever Deano's just said. His gaze lingers on my face. I feel my cheeks flushing and glance down at the yellow sneakers he's wearing. When I look back at him, he's frowning at what's in my arms.

"Jack told me what's going on," he says. "You all right? About your dad and all?"

I nod. "I'm OK."

I want to say something that will keep him standing there, in front of me, while Jack and the rest of them go to their classes. For one stupid second, I think about telling Crowy about the swan and running around the lake and about the wind lifting me from the track. I want him to stay and talk to me, and look at me like Harry does.

But he doesn't. He nods at me, once, then peels off with the rest of them, heading toward the library.

I walk to art class by myself. Mrs. Diver sees me coming and pulls me aside.

"Are you OK to talk about your project today?" she asks.

I hold up the muddied wings. "It's not finished."

"Wow, you made a model already." She smiles. "It's huge!" She frowns as she tries to figure out what it is. "Just give us an update of what you're doing and that will be fine."

I take my seat next to Sophie and listen to the others talk. Most of them are doing really simple models, like Matt, who is making a sort of parachute by sticking material over a tissue box and attaching it to a basket underneath. No one else's model is as complicated as mine; nothing comes close. And no one else has finished.

No one speaks about their project for very long and soon I'm the only one in the class who hasn't said anything. Mrs. Diver looks over at me.

"Do you want to tell us about yours, Isla?" she asks. "There's no pressure."

I know my model is loads better than everyone else's, but I'm still nervous. I just wish I'd had time to clean it up. I walk to the front of the class. Already I can hear people whispering. I unfold each wing and stretch them out on Mrs. Diver's desk. Bits of reed and mud tumble out. The wings are no longer beautiful and white; instead the feathers crumple inward. The harness is dirty, too. I feel a lump in my throat as I look at it all. All that hard work Granddad did, and I've ruined the model in one night. It's so much worse than I'd expected. I stare down at the wings for ages, trying to figure out how to fix them. Then Mrs. Diver clears her throat and I realize the whole class is staring at me. I swallow slowly, take a breath.

"My flying model is based on swans' wings. I tried to make a kind of bird-wing flying harness for a human to wear."

I hold up my flying model, only it's hard to make the wings stretch out without me being inside the harness, and they flop forward. Loose feathers float to the table. I definitely hear someone laugh this time.

Jordan yells out, "What did you kill to make that?"

I press my hands to the wings. "It was stuffed," I say. "Dead already."

"Did you drag it from the town dump?"

When I look back at the class, they are staring at me like I'm insane. The boys in the back are laughing, sticking their hands into their armpits and flapping their arms like wings. It's horrible standing up there with only my scruffy, muddy flying model that doesn't look as impressive as I hoped it would. Jordan's right: It does look like something I got out of the garbage, or worse . . . like a bird I dragged out of a lake. My throat goes tight. I can feel my mouth jamming together, and I can't say what I want to say about the wires and how they move individual feathers. I can't say anything about how amazing it all is. I just stare out at the class, clasping my wings tighter and tighter.

"Bird killer," Jordan says.

Mrs. Diver comes to my rescue in the end, bustling up to the front and ushering me to sit down.

"I think it's very impressive," she says. "And we'll hear more about it later."

People tease me all day. They say nasty things about how I must have chopped up a swan.

"I thought you loved birds," Matt hisses as he brushes past me in the corridor.

Even Sophie doesn't hang out with me. On our free period, she says she's going to the library to research something. I sit on a wall outside and keep checking my phone, but Mum hasn't called. Maybe that means Dad is OK now. It's strange, but I almost want her to call just so I can get out of here.

At lunch I walk to the soccer field. Anything has got to be better than hanging around near the idiots from my class. It probably doesn't help that the wings are too big to fit in my locker and I have to carry them everywhere. I walk past Matt and Jordan and they start making clucking noises at me. That does it. I turn around, wanting to yell . . . just wanting to say something that will shut them up. But the lump is in my throat again and I can't do it. I just gape at them, and they only laugh more.

I start jogging. It feels as though everyone in the school is watching me, laughing at the wings in my arms. I keep my head down, not meeting anyone's gaze. I pull the phone from my pocket and check it again, almost crashing into someone as I do . . . but nothing.

Jack's friends are down near one of the goals. There are about six boys including Jack passing the ball between them, and a few girls watching on the side. Jess is there, too. She laughs as Jack stops the ball with his shoulder, then flicks it across to Crowy. Crowy flips the ball down to his knee, grinning as he shows off. None of them notice me.

I dump the wings at the side and run onto the field. I jog over to Jack, but he just calls to Crowy to pass him the ball back.

"What are you doing here?" he hisses.

I stare at him blankly. "You said you'd be here."

He flashes a quick look in the direction of the girls as he receives the ball, then balances it on his foot. "Has something happened with Dad?"

"Mum hasn't called."

He rolls the ball onto the grass, but doesn't pass it to me. He flicks it up to his knee as Jess looks at him. I understand, then, why he doesn't want me to play.

"You're trying to show off," I say. "For her."

He stops to glare at me, boots the ball over to Crowy. "Don't be an idiot."

Crowy stops the ball with his chest, then rolls it down to his knee. He bounces it from one knee to the other. The girls clap, someone yells for him to get his gear off. They start up a chant. Jack jogs over to Crowy, leaves me standing by myself on the edge of the field. I kick at the grass, sending little chunks of it into the air.

The girls' chants get louder as Crowy starts pretending that he's stripping for them and his shirt edges up around his stomach. He doesn't look over to me at all, doesn't even acknowledge I'm here. He just keeps acting up for these girls. I keep kicking at the grass. I want to run over, grab the ball, and play for real. I want Crowy to stop being an idiot. I look across at Jack, but he's laughing as much as the rest of them. For some reason, that makes me madder than anything. How can he laugh and be silly when Dad's lying sick in a hospital bed?

So I run at him. I don't even bother with a proper tackle; instead I use the whole of my leg to knock him sideways.

"Hey, calm down," I hear Crowy say.

I don't listen. I stick my arm out and push it against Jack's chest. He stumbles a bit, but he doesn't fall. Somehow he manages to keep hold of the ball.

"What are you doing?" he whispers.

"Just give me the ball."

"Why should I?"

"Cos you're being stupid with it."

He frowns as he looks at me. "You're off your rocker."

"I just want to play."

I push both my arms into Jack's chest, try to push him away. I dig at the ball. But he's right there, leaning into me, using his weight to shove me toward the grass. My feet trip over his. I'm starting to fall when my phone rings.

I hit the ground with a thud. Jack's leaning over me immediately, his fingers grasping at my coat, trying to grab at the phone in my pocket.

"Get off me!" I yell.

He's pulling my arms, yanking me to my feet. "It's Mum. Answer it!"

"Stop it!" I roll over on the grass, away from him. "She's calling *me*, not you."

"Just answer the damn phone." He's still grabbing. He doesn't even care that he's hurting me.

I dig in my pocket. My fingers can't grasp the phone quick enough. Crowy's there, too, now, behind Jack, looking from me to him. He's still got a grin on his face, thinking this is all just a stupid joke. The phone stops then.

Jack kicks a loose bit of dirt at me. "That's your fault!"

I kneel on the grass and glare at him. "You don't care," I say. "You'd rather show off to your *girlfriend* than care about Dad."

Jack's face clouds over. He starts forward as if he's about to hit me. Then the phone starts again. I take a few steps away to answer, and Crowy gets in the way of Jack and starts murmuring something to him. Mum's face flashes up on my screen.

"How's Dad?" I ask.

There's a pause. My body goes stiff, and I'm sure my heartbeat stops for a second. Jack and Crowy step closer, crowd around. I don't move a muscle, not even to push them away. I hear Mum take a breath.

"He's got worse," she says quietly. "Shall I come and get you?"

I grab my wings and run. I don't look back at Jack or his friends, just run across the field with my head down. Of course, Jack comes after me.

"Mum will be at the bus stop in ten minutes," I yell back to him. "It's up to you if you come."

He turns then, shouts something to his friends. I keep running. Past the music wing, through the teachers' parking lot, and past the school office. I don't even bother to stop and tell anyone I'm leaving.

We sit in the bus shelter, at opposite ends. Jack doesn't say sorry for pushing me over. It starts to rain again.

When Mum pulls up, she's got black lines under her eyes from where her mascara has run.

"What happened?" Jack asks.

"His heart rate's increased and he's not responding to antibiotics." She leans over to wipe a smudge of mud from

Jack's cheek. "They're almost sure now it's an infection."

"Do they know how he got it?" I ask quietly.

"They're doing tests to find out."

We're silent. The only sound is the windshield wipers on the glass. I push the wing model off my lap, shove it away from me. I remember the way everyone was laughing at it in school, and suddenly I hate it. It hasn't helped the swan to fly. And it hasn't made Dad get better, either. It might even have made him worse.

Mum explains how the doctor is also worried that Dad's body might be rejecting the new valve.

"If that's the case, then this is really serious," she whispers.

I just hope Dad's valve came from a strong pig. I hope it was a pig that ran and ran all day and never got tired. But what kind of pig does that? I rub at my arms where Jack grabbed me, pull back my shirt to see that my skin's already turned pink.

Mum edges the car into the traffic and we drive out of the town. We're almost at the hospital when the flock appears. The swans fly over the road, right in front of us, and head back the other way. I turn around to watch them. Like last time, they seem to be heading for the fields near Granddad's house.

"I bet Dad would like to know where they go," I say. "It might cheer him up."

Mum glances at me in the rearview mirror. "Not now, Isla."

The parking lot is really full and Mum has to drive around and around. Each lap seems to take forever. In the end she parks the car right up against the fence in an area that isn't really a space.

"That'll have to do," she says.

I leave the wings on the seat. I grasp the fence with my fingertips and listen for swans. I can only hear rain. Maybe the swan on the lake has already left; maybe she's joined the flock I just saw flying over the highway. Why hasn't Harry texted to tell me? It's been almost two days since he kissed me, and I haven't heard a thing.

I run after Mum and Jack. The elevator takes forever. My hands are tight fists in my pockets, squeezing a heartbeat rhythm. A whole team of nurses gets in at Harry's floor, but I don't recognize any of them from his ward. I hope he's all right. Perhaps his phone battery has run out and he hasn't been able to charge it. Perhaps he's embarrassed about what happened the other night. I dig my nails into my skin until it hurts, and hope he hasn't got sicker. I'll visit him after this; go and make sure. There's that fluttery feeling in my chest again as I think about seeing him.

When the elevator doors open on the ICU's floor, the nurse who was looking after Dad last time comes straight up to us.

"Still the same," she says, looking at Mum's expression. Her eyes linger over me and Jack. "You'll have to go in one at a time, I'm afraid, and only five minutes each."

"I'm first," Jack says. I hate him for that.

Mum and Jack put plastic bags over their shoes again and go into the room. I try sitting on the chair beside the desk, but I'm too restless. I pace the corridor instead. I think I can remember waiting in a corridor like this once before Dad was sick, with all of us together. I have a bunch of hazy memories that don't make sense. Mum with her arms around Dad's waist. Saying good-bye to Nan. Seeing Granddad cry. I stop pacing as I remember it. It shocks me even now to think of Granddad with tears on his face. Maybe my mind has twisted the memory and it was really Dad who was crying.

I go back to the chair beside the desk. Why are Mum and Jack taking so long? Five minutes, the nurse said. I check my watch, see that it's been seven minutes already. I can't wait any longer. When the nurse leaves the desk, I step quietly toward Dad's room.

Like last time, the blue curtains are drawn around most of the beds. But not Dad's. Even from here I can see Jack and Mum, leaning over him. I take a few steps forward so that I can see Dad, too. When I do, I freeze. His eyes are shut. There's a mask over his mouth and nose, exactly like the one he had on in the ambulance. He looks so sick, even sicker than how he looked that first day. It's as if he's fading away, merging into the whiteness of his bedsheets. I stop breathing for a moment. I think I'm about to black out. I have to step backward.

Mum hears me. She frowns as she turns. Opens her mouth to say something. I already know what it's going to be. Something about the infection Dad's got. Something about it being all my fault. Dad is going to die. It's going to be just like it was with Nan.

I claw myself away from her. I don't want to hear her words. Someone grabs my shoulders, tries to stop me, but I elbow them away. There's a strange noise coming from my throat. I don't know whether it's a word or a cry or something else entirely. Mum comes toward me. I dodge her, dodge everyone. I get out of the ward and run straight into a gurney. I push it to the side to get past. Now Jack is shouting something after me. I block it. I don't want to know. I don't want to know if it's all my fault. I don't want to think about it. But I can't help it. I can't think about anything else as I skid through the corridors. Dad's pale white face. Our family with only three. Granddad crying again. I have to go, have to get out.

I take the stairs two at a time, jump down the last few. I bolt through the parking lot. I'm just running; my feet are leading me. I don't know what else to do. I pass Mum's car, tumble through the tear in the fence. Slip on a pile of leaves. It feels like there's a hole opening up somewhere inside me. It feels like I'm about to fall in. I have to keep running.

She's waiting. Somehow I knew she would be. She swims toward me, comes right up to the bank. I want to bury myself in her feathers. I want to lie across her back and leave with her when she flies. She understands, I can feel it. Her gaze is on me, drawing me in. Her eyes are darker than coal dust. She hisses gently.

A wind starts up, sending my hair across my face. I lean forward, into it, let the wind hold me up. The swan moves her head up and down. She beats her wings against the water's surface and I know exactly what she wants to do. I want it, too.

I start to run. Down the track. The swan keeps pace on the water. She draws ahead, pulling me on. I slide over patches of frozen ground, stretch out my arms to steady myself. I feel my heart thudding in my chest. I wish I could swap it with Dad's so that he could have the healthy heart. It keeps beating, stronger and stronger. I shut my eyes for a second. Run blind. I feel the gravelly texture of the track. Smell the dampness of the lake.

I hear the swan beside me, honking and whooping. She's about to fly. I lengthen my stride. Water spins out from her wings and lands on my cheeks. I beat my arms, too, hoping to encourage her. I wish I was wearing the flying harness. But she doesn't need it. As I turn to watch, the lake drops away from her feet. And then . . . up, UP. She's flying.

I watch her stretch forward, her beak pointing toward the

sky. I see the wind rippling her feathers, the muscles moving in her neck. I hear the whirring of her wings as she climbs higher and higher.

I run behind her. I'm only going to follow her until she starts to draw away from me. But she stays there, flying low, only about fifteen feet above my head. It's as if she wants me to come with her. So I do. I run past the end of the lake and past the trees. There's a pathway, leading over a stile and out across the fields. I follow it. Leap the fence. Now that I'm running like this, following her, it feels like I can keep running forever. I look up at the swan. She's watching from above, keeping pace with me exactly . . . deliberately going slowly so I can follow. I don't know whether she's leading me or I'm leading her.

Then I remember something. This is the direction that the swan flock was heading this afternoon. I dig my toes into the ground and go faster. Suddenly, it all seems so simple. I need to take her there, I need to lead her back to her flock. If I can't help Dad, then at least I can help her.

I head across the fields, hope I'm going in the right direction. It gets darker as I run. The lights from the hospital and the highway begin to fade as I go farther into the countryside. But I can still see the swan above me. The white glow of her wings stands out clearly against the darkening sky.

An ache starts in my chest and spreads into my shoulders. But I keep going. Even when the air thickens into mist. It clogs my nose and mouth and makes my clothes feel heavy. It makes the lights from the highway disappear entirely. There's a shriek. *Her.* I look up. Everything's black. Only the damp feeling on my eyeballs tells me my eyes are open, not closed. My swan has disappeared.

I run into the mist and darkness. I listen for her shrieks to lead me on. She's in front of me now. I'm going only by sound, trusting the swan not to lead me into a lake or a fence. I shut my eyes, then open them again. There's no difference. It's too black. I don't know which way is ahead or behind, up or down. I'm running in a black hole. Or maybe I'm flying, soaring behind her.

I press my hand to my chest to feel my heart. It's beating strongly. I keep my hand there and think of Dad, running across that field two weeks ago . . . It must have been near here. I wish I could have caught up with him. I wish I could have grabbed him and told him to stop.

My swan shrieks again. I turn my body toward the noise. I start to see flickers of light between the clouds. Stars. There's movement up ahead. And something else. Coming out of the mist is a sound. The sound I've been waiting to hear. It's a crying, low and eerie. It's the sound of a flock.

As we get closer, I see their shadows. The air smells different; it's damper and fresher somehow. We're near a lake. I hear the birds start to murmur as they welcome us. The swan above me shrieks and shrieks. I've done it.

I've found her flock! I slow down. My legs feel so heavy; my shoulders stiff. I don't know whether it's because of the mist, but I'm suddenly light-headed. Drifting. It feels like I'm flying with my swan toward the water.

I don't see the stump. I go right over the top of it and tumble toward the lake and the shadowy swans. My head hits something hard. Stones scrape my skin. All I can hear is the shrieking of birds.

Then, whiteness. Feathers. *Her.* Everything starts to fade. And I'm sinking down . . .

Down into the wet earth and the pond weed. Cold travels along my veins and turns them to ice. If I move now, I'll crack.

The wind howls like a wild thing. Everything goes numb.

Blackness.

Cold.

Sleep.

My swan comes back. She brings others. They whoop softly and their feathers touch me on all sides. I press my head against them, bury my nose into that smell of feather. They don't move away. I shut my eyes and let them take my weight. For a moment, I imagine it's Dad I'm leaning on, and his arms are tight around me. Mum's on the other side. I can almost smell her perfume. And Harry's there, too, holding my hand.

I feel myself moving. A push forward and the swans take me with them. They hold me with their wings and I start to run. We leap together in huge strides, their out-stretched wings bearing my weight. I leap and leap, forcing myself to keep up with them. The swans whoop, getting louder and louder as we run. As we start to take off I stumble, but the swans are beside me, supporting me, lift-ing me higher. I feel weightless, as if I've left my body far behind. The swans stretch out across the sky, their wings carrying me into the wind, whirring and beating all around.

They're singing.

There's something warm and wet in my ear. Then it touches my cheek. Something is nuzzling me, nudging me awake. I try my eyelids, manage to open them. There's a black snout. A pink tongue. A snuffling sound.

A dog.

A hand reaches down and drags it away.

"Get out of there, Dig!"

I know that voice. I blink, try to see where it's coming from. Everything's too blurry. Too dark. I try moving my head. I'm cold and stiff. The pink tongue tries to lick me. Then Granddad is there, leaning over me. His eyes are wide gray pools. There's a thick scarf around his neck.

"Stay still. I'll help you."

He presses my shoulders, and I feel the cold, jagged ground beneath me.

"The swans," I murmur.

Granddad leans over me again, smiles a little. "Yes," he says. "I know. They came back. You did, too."

I feel my head sinking down. His arm slides under my neck. He lifts me up. And suddenly I'm weightless again, floating and flying. I look up at the night sky and the stars sparkle like sequins.

I can smell tomato soup. I open my eyes. I'm lying on Granddad's couch. He's in the armchair across from me, watching me carefully. He leans forward as I try to focus.

"How are you feeling?" he says.

I start to sit up and a sharp pain shoots down my spine. I gasp. Granddad's there immediately, helping to make me comfortable against the cushions.

"I've checked you over," he murmurs. "There's nothing broken. I called your mother when I found you."

For a second I want to reach forward and touch his face, just to know that he's real. I can't hear the swans.

"What happened?" I say.

Granddad puts his hand behind my shoulder, supporting me. His hands feel like the swans' wings, pushing me up. I glance out the window and see the white-blue sky. There are no birds.

"You were running," Granddad murmurs. ". . . away from the hospital. I heard the swans arrive so I went outside to see what was going on. I found you. You've been sleeping ever since."

Granddad is watching me carefully. There's something about his expression that seems important somehow. Then I get it.

Dad.

I sit up quickly and feel pain in my legs and arms. Granddad tries to push me back against the couch, but I won't let him. Not until I know.

"What happened?" I whisper. "At the hospital? Is Dad . . . ?"

I remember the mask over his mouth. Mum's expression. That feeling of emptiness. I swallow the sick feeling in my throat as I wait for Granddad's words.

Granddad touches my chin, forces me to look at him. "Your father . . . ," he begins, ". . . they think he'll pull through. He's responding now."

I keep looking at Granddad's face. At that moment, he looks just like . . .

"Dad . . . ," I try to say. "I thought . . . I thought he was . . ."

I feel the wave in my throat, the tears welling in my eyes. Granddad's eyes water up, too.

"I know," he says. "I thought that as well."

He hugs me tight. His sweater smells like woodsmoke

and fried food, and his body feels stiff. I wonder when he last really hugged someone.

"We'd better get you to the hospital," he says.

He leans away. He sits back on his heels and wipes his hands over his face.

"Do you want to go now?" he asks. "Or do you want to lie here a little longer?"

"Let's go now."

He puts his arm around my waist as I stand. He half carries me to his car. It's so cold outside, colder than it's been for days. Our breath is like vapor trails. I make Granddad stop for a moment so I can hear the swans. I can't see them from here, but I know where they are: Granddad's lake, only a hundred yards away. Granddad turns his head and listens with me. I shut my eyes. Is my swan there? When I look back at Granddad, he's still listening.

"They haven't been back for six years," he murmurs.

"I know. Not since Nan . . ."

The words catch in my throat and I look up at Granddad. He nods.

"Yes. Not since then." He studies the sky above the lake and shakes his head a little. "It's what I wanted her to see, before she . . ." He struggles for words, coughs suddenly. "She shouldn't have been looking at four walls when she went. She wanted to be outside."

He doesn't hold my gaze, but glances ahead to his car

instead. Then he starts walking toward it. I let him lead me. There will be time to go back and see the swans another day. Once a flock finds a roosting ground, they'll stay for a while; Dad's told me that many times. I wonder about my swan, floating with the rest of them. I'm so glad she's here.

Granddad starts the car and drives slowly. There's no one on the roads; no one else has woken up yet. I watch the fields blur past, the fields I must have run through last night. Frost makes them glisten and sparkle. There are starlings bobbing on the electrical wires. I wonder how she did it, how she flew. Was it me? Did I lead her? Or did she suddenly figure out where her flock was and need to get to them? But then why did she take me?

I stretch across the gear stick and rest my head on Granddad's shoulder. "You're coming with me this time," I say. "Into the hospital. Dad needs all of us."

I make Granddad park the car, then wait for him to get out and join me. He takes a handkerchief and wipes it around his face.

"I won't stay long," he says.

We walk in together. I keep my hand inside the crook of his elbow. He coughs and blows his nose and dawdles. We stop to wait for the elevators.

"You're not going to disappear again, are you?" I ask. "When we get to Dad's ward?"

Granddad holds his handkerchief to his nose and blows loudly. He looks around at everyone else waiting for the elevators.

"I'll stay," he says. "Just for a bit."

I lead him down the corridor to Intensive Care. Mum is waiting outside the door. I brace myself, wait for her to grab me by the shoulders and start telling me off. But instead, she hugs me. I breathe in the flowery smell of her cardigan.

"I'm sorry," she says. "I should have told you more of what was going on. You ran away so fast, I didn't have time to explain." She pushes me back to look at my face. "Jack and I were worried."

It's my turn to apologize. I look away, guilty. "Dad's OK, though?" I ask.

She nods. "He's still sick, Isla, but the medication is working now."

"But last night, he . . . ?"

"I know." She brushes her fingers through my hair. "I was scared, too. But they've added in some different antibiotics, and he's responding. The infection's not as bad."

"Was it because of me?" I say. "Because I went to visit him after I'd been at the lake?"

She shakes her head quickly. "It's just something that happens," she says. "One of those things, could have been anything." Mum moves her hand to my forehead and pushes away my frown. "It's no one's fault."

Jack's behind her. His eyes are reddish and small, as if he hasn't slept. There's a bit of twig in his hair and a small leaf stuck to his sweater.

"Where've you been?" I ask.

"Went looking for you, you idiot."

"To the lake?"

He nods. He's looking at me strangely, a smile playing on his lips.

"What did you see?"

"I saw you running really fast and a swan chasing after you. Then I lost you."

I smile back at him. "Couldn't keep up?"

He frowns. "You just had a head start." He keeps frowning as he watches me. "You OK now?" he asks.

I shrug. "If Dad is."

I hear Mum talking softly to Granddad, thanking him for finding me. He's brushing away her gratitude.

"It was the swans," he says. "I wouldn't have gone out there if it hadn't been for their noise . . ."

I let his words fade out behind me as I take a step toward Dad's ward. Jack comes with me, saying something to the nurse as we pass. We walk down the center aisle of the room, past all the other patients. I see him immediately. There are tubes running into his arm and nose, but he no longer has the mask over his face. His eyes are closed. I walk up to him. He doesn't look that different to how he looked last night, still so sick. Jack comes to stand beside me.

"His temperature's down," he says. "And he's not asleep all the time."

I brush my fingers lightly against Dad's arm. His eyes

flicker open, just for a moment. He doesn't smile, doesn't move any other part of his face, but I know he's seen me . . . knows I'm here. I place my hand on his. His skin still feels a little waxy. His fingers twitch and grip at mine.

"I've brought Granddad to see you," I say.

I don't hang around to watch Granddad go in. Instead, I go to find Harry. A nurse lets me in.

"Haven't seen you for a few days," she says.

Harry's door is open this time. He's sitting up in bed, but turned away from me and looking out the window. Granddad's green hat is still on his head. I can't see any orangey tufts of hair underneath it. My legs are shaking a bit when I take a step toward him. I think I'm nervous about how he will react to me after what happened at the lake. Maybe he regrets it; maybe he didn't want to kiss me after all. It's three days since we went down there and I've had no text message from him. But when he turns toward me, his smile is brilliant and makes his whole face shine.

"What took you so long?" he says.

My breath comes out in a rush. I don't know where to start. So I walk right up to him and sit on the edge of his bed. "I was waiting for you to text me."

He laughs and reaches forward to hug me. "That's your fault," he says, his words loud and low in my ear. "When you chucked my clothes out the window, you chucked my phone out with them." He pulls away and looks at my face. "Imagine how I explained that to my mum."

The skin over his cheeks looks stretched, and his eyebrows have almost disappeared.

"Are you OK?" I whisper. "You look kind of different."

He sighs. He lifts his hand to the hat. "You ready?" he asks.

He pulls it off. Underneath, he's bald. His skin is so white and his head looks suddenly huge.

"Shaved it yesterday," he says. "I was fed up with it coming out."

I reach up and touch his head. It feels so soft. When I brush my fingers along it, I can feel the tiniest fuzz of hair.

"It's like fur," I say.

His eyes look enormous without his scruffy hair, brighter than ever. He moves to put his hat back on but I stop his hand.

"It suits you," I say.

He smiles crookedly. "Now you're just being nice. You don't have to say that."

"I'm not. You look like some sort of creature, something wild."

"Like a rat, you mean?" He looks down at his blankets. "Some sort of bald mole?"

I wait for him to look back to me. "No." I touch his head again, I love the way his skin is so soft against my fingertips. "You look beautiful."

The words are out before I realize it. I freeze, my hand still on his head. Already I can feel my cheeks coloring from embarrassment.

But he moves toward me and kisses me softly.

"Thanks," he says.

He clasps his arms around me and hugs me for ages. I rest my head down against his shoulder. "When's your transplant?" I ask.

"About two weeks' time. They're bringing bone marrow across from Germany. Crazy, isn't it?" I feel him tense beneath me.

"What will happen?"

He shifts so he can see me when he speaks. "They'll use drugs to kill off all my bone marrow and cancer cells, then they'll hook up this German person's bone marrow and feed it through here." He touches the place on his chest where I saw the two tubes coming out. "Hopefully my body will like it. Otherwise . . ." His words disappear as he glances away from me.

I shudder suddenly. "How long?" I whisper. "How long have you got if your body doesn't like it?"

He keeps looking away from me. "I don't know, really, maybe not long at all."

He looks so sad that I want to make him smile.

"You know what they say about German bone marrow?" I say.

"What's that?"

"It's the best! It's tougher and stronger than anything. It's like putting titanium in your spine. You'll be as strong as Wolverine."

He smiles. "Better be." His voice is whispery. He wants to get more words out, but he can't. It's enough, though. I can guess what he wants to say. It's what I'm thinking, too. There's only a fifty percent chance; only half a chance all this will work. He might even die on the day it happens. I lean right into him and wrap my arms around his chest. I can feel the tubes through his pajamas, resting against my cheek, but I bury into him anyway and breathe in that pine tree smell of his. I feel his chest trembling, as if he's trying to hold back a whole avalanche of tears. After a while, he relaxes. He moves his face so that it's resting on my hair and I feel his breath against my ear. We stay like that for ages.

It's Harry who moves first. He pushes me off him, wipes his hand across his nose.

"So, tell me," he says quietly. "You went to the lake again, didn't you?"

"How did you know?"

"There's something about you when you've been down there. It's like a sparkle or something. It's infectious. And anyway, the swan's not there anymore and I figured you had something to do with it."

So I tell him. "I found her flock," I say. "I led her to them. Or she led me."

I tell him about running across the fields and collapsing near the lake. I even tell him of the dream I had when I took off with the swans.

"It felt so real," I whisper. "It felt like I was flying. It felt as though the swans flew with me to Granddad's."

His eyes dart over my face. "It wouldn't be the first time you flew." He smiles and I know he's remembering what happened on the lake that night. He turns to the window. "Now that she's found her flock, do you think she'll stay there? I mean, will she ever come back?"

His eyes are skimming across the water, watching.

"Maybe. Will you miss her?"

He shrugs. "What else do I have to look at now?"

He shuffles over on his mattress so I can squeeze up next to him. We both look out at the water.

"I'll visit you," I say.

"Promise?" He turns to look at me. "You're not just going to forget me once your dad gets better?"

I raise my eyebrows. "As if!"

Harry leans back against the wall. "How is he, anyway?"

So I tell him about that, too. I explain how I thought Dad was dying last night. It's so easy talking to Harry. It's as if I can tell him anything at all. He holds my hand tightly as I speak.

"Promise me something else?" he says.

"What?"

"Promise we'll see that swan again before I go into isolation?"

I look at his bright eyes. "What if she doesn't come back here? What if she stays on Granddad's lake?"

"Then I'll ask my doctor if I can come with you, just once . . . just one afternoon."

"Will they let you?"

He grins. "Maybe if I beg and plead and say it's my dying wish."

"Hey!" I pinch his arm. "Don't even joke about that stuff."

Then I hold up my little finger and tell him to wrap his little finger around mine and shake a fairy's handshake.

"I promise," I say softly.

Harry's face crumples into a laugh as he tries to understand me. He won't let me release my little finger from his.

"I'll hold you to it, you know."

And I hope more than anything that he does.

I meet them at the hospital café. Jack's fiddling with his paper coffee cup, tearing bits off the top of it. Granddad's there, too, but he doesn't have a coffee in front of him. I can tell by how tense he looks that he's itching to get going.

"Did you see Dad?" I ask.

He nods, glancing around at the other customers. "He looks better than I thought. The doctors are more skilled, this time."

He gets up quickly, his chair squeaking on the concrete. He raises his eyebrows at Mum. "See you then, Cath."

"Bye, Martin." She smiles, and I can see how grateful she is that Granddad came today. She looks at me, slightly amazed.

"Well done," she says. "He really would do anything for you."

She pushes across a cup of hot chocolate to me, and explains what happens next.

"They'll monitor Dad carefully for the next few days," she says. "Just to make sure he keeps getting better. They'll help him to get used to his new valve."

"When does he come out?" Jack asks.

Mum leans over to gather up the bits of coffee cup he's spread on the table. "He'll be in the hospital a while longer. They have to make sure he's fully recovering first."

We walk to the car. It's parked in a different place from where Mum left it last night, so I guess they must have been home in between, or else they came to Granddad's when I was still asleep. My flying model is still in there, though.

I stretch out across the backseat, use the model as a pillow. I tilt my head so I can look at the sky. My whole body is still aching from last night, my muscles throbbing from the run. I shut my eyes and let my head sink into the wings. I breathe in that smell of lake.

I visit Dad every day. It's not long before they take the tubes out of his nose. Then he's back in his old ward and eating the regular hospital food again. We bring him little treats each day, too. Mum lets me choose things for him from the hospital shop. Dad wolfs them all down, even though the nurses say he shouldn't be this hungry yet.

"You're like a trash can," I tell him. "We just keep chucking things inside you."

I watch Dad getting better. His breathing is heavy and raggedy at first, but it becomes normal again after a day or two. Then he's well enough to get out of his bed. His steps are slow and shaky, and he has to grasp the corner of his bedside table and wait a moment to get his breath back, but he does it. He walks the whole way around his ward. The next day he walks around it without stopping.

I help him back into his bed. Plump up his pillows for

him. He's got thinner since he's been here. I wonder how long it will be before he's properly Dad-shaped again. I think about the swan on her new lake. She must be changing shape, too, getting fuller and fatter in preparation for her migration home. Her gray baby feathers will have fully transformed into white adult ones by now. It's only Harry who doesn't get healthier, and his feathers don't grow back.

I visit him every time I see Dad, and sit with him on his bed. We look out at the lake. The reeds have turned straw yellow and there are huge puddles on the track. He's gone quieter without the swan. He says it's because he misses her, but I know he's worried about his transplant. He laces his fingers, crossing and uncrossing his thumbs. I wish I could smooth the frown from his face.

One evening after I get home from the hospital, I take the wing model and spread its wings across the kitchen table. It's art tomorrow, and Mrs. Diver wants us to present our finished projects. I'm dreading it. I haven't done any more work on mine and the rest of my class will only make fun of me again. It'll be awful. But Mum offers to help me clean up the feathers, and she never even asks how they got so dirty in the first place. So I let her.

She finds disinfectant under the sink and stain remover in the laundry room. I tip capfuls into bowls and pour water on top. We dip rags in and swirl them around. Then we rub gently at the wings. Some of the mud comes out right away and makes the water brown. We keep rubbing until every single mark has gone from the feathers and they change from brownish gray to white. Then Mum finds a needle and thread and helps sew up the gaps where feathers have fallen out. I try on the harness. Mum gasps as I spread the wings out behind me.

"It's magnificent," she says.

I move my fingers and rotate my arms so that some of the feathers tilt. Others are too damaged to move. But it's still pretty amazing.

"Turn around," she says.

So I do. One of my wings gets caught against the glasses' cabinet and the other one knocks over the lamp. Mum dives for it. She puts the lamp back in place, then helps me fold up the wing model.

"You don't have to worry about tomorrow," she says. "Just show them this; show them how all the wires work and how you made it. They'll be amazed. And if they're not, they're idiots."

I blink at her. "Idiots?"

"Yeah." She helps unbuckle the straps across my chest. "I think what you've built is brilliant. Dad does, too. And, by the sounds of it . . ." She stops to poke me in the ribs. ". . . so does Harry."

I feel my cheeks blushing and I know Mum sees.

"So," she says, "if *we* all love what you've created, what have you got to worry about?"

rs. Diver taps her pen, getting everyone's attention. It's my turn to do my presentation. She watches my face carefully as I stand.

"You OK?" she mouths.

I nod. I take my flying model to the front of the class. Already I can hear people whispering and someone, probably Jordan, muffling a laugh. Mrs. Diver shushes everyone and tells me to begin. I swallow and try not to look at the bunch of boys in the back row who are still flapping their arms about and pretending to be birds. I look at Mrs. Diver's picture of da Vinci and pretend I'm just talking to him.

"Leonardo da Vinci studied bird wings when he researched his flying machines," I say. "He drew sketches of how he could connect wings to a man's body. So, when I found a stuffed swan in my granddad's barn, I thought that my flying model would be a bit like this . . . a kind of flying machine that used real bird wings."

I return my gaze to the class. The boys in the back are still grinning like crazy, just waiting to make bird noises again. Some of the kids in the front are doodling on their workbooks, not paying attention to my presentation; others are passing notes. I step into the harness. I get Mrs. Diver to help tighten the leather straps across my chest and fasten the Velcro loops. There's a few hushed murmurs. The kids in the front have noticed. But others still don't have a clue that I've just attached a pair of wings to my back. So I bend my elbows and bring my fists toward my chest, then I force them back out again. The wires are stiff, but I manage it. I open my wings, and start beating them. The air they create sends a stack of papers floating toward the floor. They make textbook pages flap and turn. I move my fingers so that the feathers angle and separate. I roll my shoulders and the wings flutter behind me.

The class goes quiet. Heads turn toward me.

"I observed how a whooper swan used her wings," I say. "I made sketches."

Mrs. Diver holds up the pencil drawings I did of the swan on the lake. She nods her head in approval. I keep beating the wings slowly.

"I thought that if I learned how a swan flew, I could work out which parts of the stuffed wings I'd need to move to copy it."

I arch my back and the wings arch with me. I beat my arms a little faster and the feathers start to make a whirring noise. I have to raise my voice as I speak.

"I learned that a swan can feel the wind against each one of its feathers. It knows how to rotate its wings so that the wind rushes over them in just the right way."

I beat faster, angling my wrists and turning the feathers as I do. I send project sheets spinning to the floor. Corners of posters come away from the wall. I'm good at this now. I don't even need to look at the wings to know which feathers I'm moving. I turn sideways and send a wave of air out over the class, making school ties flip. My skin tingles. I want to be back at the lake, running with my swan.

I turn to the front.

"But a swan can't fly alone, not for any great distance. The air is too dense and the wind too strong for only one pair of wings. They need the flock."

I start to beat a little slower for my final few words.

"Only with a flock do swans have the strength to make migrations happen. And that's why Leonardo da Vinci's flying machine, based on bird wings, would never work . . . not really. You'd need other swans taking off and flying with you . . . you'd need to share their flight, too."

I slow my arms, lift my fingers to put the feathers back into place. I look back at the class. Everyone is watching now. Sophie is leaning forward over her desk, grinning at me. There are some people gathered in the corridor, too, looking in the classroom window and wondering what the heck I'm doing. I think I see Jack. I pull the Velcro with my teeth and undo it. I unbuckle the leather straps and step out from the harness. Mrs. Diver is watching openmouthed, totally impressed.

On Saturday, Jack and I stay at home and make the house look nice for Dad. We make a huge *Welcome Home* sign and I draw birds on the edge of it. It's totally corny, but Dad will like it. About half an hour before Mum and Dad are due to arrive, Jess shows up. Jack runs for the door, then brings her inside.

"I thought she could help us decorate," he says.

There's an awkward moment where Jess is standing in the hall and I'm in the kitchen and we're just sort of looking at each other. Then Jack chucks a bag of balloons in her direction and she gets to work. He wraps his arms around her waist and lifts her onto a chair so she can help pin up the sign. It's easy to see how much he's into her. When we're finished, we sit around the table.

"Come to the park with us sometimes," she says. "We need a few more girls."

He mock punches her arm. "You wanna be friends with my little sister?" But then he laughs.

I think about sitting with their group on top of the playground castle, wonder about bringing Harry, too, when he's better.

"OK," I say.

When Jess goes, Jack and I sit on the front step to wait for Dad. He keeps looking across at me, waiting for me to say something.

"She's nice," I say, laughing. "I can't believe she wants to be *your* girlfriend!"

He gets his arm around my neck and scoops me in a headlock. "Why would I care what you think?"

But he does. He wouldn't have brought her over otherwise. Then Mum's car pulls up and we go to help Dad get out. He's weak and pale and still so thin, but he's smiling. Jack makes pig noises as he helps Dad to the door.

"Jack," Mum warns.

"But he's right," I say. "Dad's half pig now, half animal."

Then, as Dad comes into the kitchen, he sees our *Welcome Home* sign and our balloons, and his face crumples. He starts crying and smiling at the same time.

I keep my arms clasped around his waist; I'm just so glad he's back.

*T*he following Friday I get a text message from Harry.

I can go find the swan! But have to take Mum, a nurse,
and go in an ambulance.

I smile then, and text back:

Tomorrow?

I can't believe he managed to get permission. Maybe he did pull the "I might be dead in a week" card.

We go the next morning. Dad waits in the car while Mum and I meet Harry at the hospital entrance. He's in a wheelchair with loads of blankets wrapped around him, and he's still wearing Granddad's hat. There's a lady with him who has bright hazel eyes and the same gingery hair. It can only be his mum. She knows who I am immediately.

"I've heard lots about you," she says, winking at Harry, who turns redder than a tomato.

Mum laughs and I know exactly what she's going to say next.

"And I've heard lots about Harry."

I groan. I walk over to Harry and let the mums talk.

"You all right?" I say, kneeling down to him.

He grins. "I get to see your swan again."

A nurse pulls up in a normal-looking car that has *ambulance* painted on the side. She wheels Harry over to it and he eases himself onto the backseat. Then she folds up the wheelchair and puts it in the trunk. His mum holds open the passenger door, then pauses.

"Why don't you come with us, Isla?"

Mum pushes me forward. "Go on," she murmurs. "Dad won't mind."

I climb in beside Harry. As soon as I'm in he grabs my hand and holds it across the backseat. It's kind of embarrassing, but Harry's mum looks out the window and pretends she hasn't noticed.

"Your skin's boiling!" I say, surprised and worried at the same time.

"It's OK. I've just got two hot water bottles on my lap," he explains. "I'm wrapped up like takeout!"

Then he leans forward to speak to the nurse. "Does this thing have sirens?"

The nurse smiles as she shakes her head. "It's not that kind of ambulance, Harry."

I'm glad about that. I don't think I ever want to be in that kind of ambulance again. I look out the back window to see Mum's car traveling behind us. Dad makes faces at us from the passenger seat, then blows us kisses.

I turn back to the front quickly, and hope Harry hasn't noticed how Dad's goofing around.

It doesn't take us long to get to Granddad's house. The hospital car goes slowly down the lane so as not to jolt Harry too much. Granddad's waiting in his driveway. His hands are clasped together as if he's a little anxious. If he notices that his hat's on Harry's head, he doesn't say anything.

"I've made a gap in the fence," he tells the nurse. "So you can get the wheelchairs through. And I've tried to flatten the ground."

Harry gets out of the car and I stand next to him while the nurse gets his wheelchair ready. I look across to see Mum getting one out of the trunk of her car, too.

"For Dad," she says, wheeling it around to the passenger seat. "Heaven forbid that we leave him behind."

The nurse laughs. "This trip is quite the mission," she says. "Hope this swan's worth it."

Harry and I exchange a look. *If only they knew.* I keep hold of his hand.

We set off across the field; Harry first, with the nurse, and me and his mum walking beside them. Mum wheels Dad a few feet behind us. Granddad brings up the rear. He's made a good track for the wheelchairs, considering the ground's so tufty and uneven, but Harry still winces as his body is bounced around.

The swans start whooping before we get there, and their noise echoes around the landscape. Harry's mum jumps when she hears it.

"That's them," Harry tells her. "That's the swans."

She looks at him curiously. "How did you get to know so much about birds?" she asks.

Then a flock of starlings shoots up from the field, their wings glinting as they all turn at once. We stop to watch them. They chatter like toys. Harry grits his teeth as the nurse moves his chair again, and his mum bends to tuck the blankets around him tighter. "We won't stay long," she says. "We'll just see the swan and go, OK?"

She keeps whispering to him, asking if he's all right. Her eyes don't move from his face.

I look over to Dad, wondering if he's OK, too, but he's managing fine. As we get closer to the water, he starts grinning. He turns around to talk to Granddad.

"There must be close to twenty of them," he says. "How do they fit on the lake?"

Granddad smiles slowly. "They manage. I chopped back some of the weeds so there's more room."

I wait for a few moments until they catch up with me.

"I'm impressed," Dad says, glancing from me over to Harry. "Bird-watching on the first date, *and* he's already met the family."

"Dad!" I glare at him to shut up.

Mum throws him a look, too. But already his eyes are on the sky, following a small bird that's flapping in bursts.

"Brambling!" he says, pointing it out to me.

I look up, catch a glimpse of orange on the bird's chest. Then I'm running ahead to show Harry.

"I've found one of your birds!" I call.

Behind me, Dad's got his binoculars out, already looking for more birds. He's talking to Granddad as he does this, telling him about the letter he's just sent to the town council about the new power lines. Granddad's murmuring in response.

The air is heavy with the smell of mud and moss, but it's not cold today. It's one of those rare winter days when the sunlight is bright and warm, and it feels like a gift.

We wheel Harry and Dad close to the lake's edge. The swans are spread out right across its surface. Harry's eyes are scanning the flock, but I've seen her already. She's right in the middle, her feathers much whiter than they were before. She looks like so many of the others, but I know it's her. She stares at me with her deep, dark eyes and, even now, I feel the pull to be with her. I know Harry is watching me.

"Is that her?" he whispers.

I nod. She leaves the flock and floats toward us. I feel the flutter in my chest as she gets closer. She looks like a mythical creature arriving out of a story. Her new feathers shine like armor. I glance at Harry, see the pinkness in his cheeks. I lean over and hug him, not caring that his mum, and my mum, and Dad are right behind us. Granddad steps up to the bank and crouches down next to me. He's got his eyes fixed on the swan, too. There's a faraway smile on his face, and I wonder if he's thinking about Nan. I don't think he's been bird-watching since she died.

It takes only a few seconds for the swan to swim to our bank. She waddles up onto it. Harry's mum starts forward and puts her hands on the wheelchair handles, but Harry waves her away.

"The swan won't hurt us," he tells her. "Believe me."

Harry's mum keeps standing there, watching anxiously. The swan stands to her full height, only a few feet away. I hear the nurse gasp, and I'm amazed, too, by how big she seems. She's grown so much in the last couple of weeks; she's matured into a full-sized swan. She steps closer and Harry's mum can't help but move the wheelchair back a little. So I walk forward to the swan instead.

The swan presses her beak against the back of my hand.

It's wet and cold. A chill goes up my arm. I stroke the top of her head and she closes her eyes. She nuzzles in toward me, gurgling at the back of her throat. She looks up at me and I can guess what she's thinking. She waddles toward the water and slips off the bank. Rising up on the surface of the lake, she beats her wings. I look across at Harry.

"Go on," he says. He's also seen the look in her eyes. He knows what it means.

Dad's nodding at me, too, the smile already on his face.

I take a few steps. The nurse and Harry's mum are going to think I'm nuts, but I don't care: I start to run. I know she'll keep up. I lengthen my stride and hear the slapping sound as she brings her feet up onto the surface of the lake. The other swans make way for her, and a mallard shoots up suddenly from the reeds. I push myself harder, the thud of my sneakers keeping in time with her feet on the water. I beat my arms up and down. The swan's feet lift from the surface and in one smooth, graceful sweep into the sky, she takes off, tucking her feet up as she goes. I feel the fluttering in my chest again, the urge to be up there with her. I keep running a little way, watching her soar higher and higher above me. One long white feather drifts all the way from the sky and lands on the ground at my feet. I bend to pick it up. It's a primary flight feather.

Then I'm running back to the group to give it to Dad.

We drop Harry back in his room. He's more tired than I've ever seen him, but he's happy. He grins every time I catch his eye.

"Don't stay long, Isla," Mum whispers.

I wrap my arms around him and plant a kiss on his neck. He leans back against his pillows and holds on to my hand.

"Thank you," he murmurs.

It feels like there's a huge lump of conversation in my chest, all this stuff I want to tell him before he goes in for his transplant. But I can't find the words to start and I just stare at him in silence. My throat goes tight as I lean forward to stroke his fuzzy head.

"I'll come back before your transplant," I say.

Two days later Mum takes me to the hospital again. I bundle my flying model in a coat and carry it in my arms. Jack comes with me. He's curious about Harry, I think, plus it means he can get a lift to soccer practice. He glances nervously from side to side as we go through the cancer ward.

"It's fine," I tell him. "It's probably the nicest ward in the hospital."

He tries not to stare at a bald kid who passes us.

None of the nurses stop me. I think they must be used to me by now. They don't even seem to mind that I have a strange-looking bundle in my arms. I keep my head down and drag Jack by the sleeve.

"Wait there a second," I tell him, leaving him in the corridor.

I don't give him a chance to refuse. I just walk straight into Harry's room and shut the door behind me. Harry's sitting up in his bed.

"I've got a present for you," I say.

I drop the bundle on his blankets. He leans forward and takes the coat away without saying a word. He gazes wide-eyed at the flying model for a few long moments, then begins to unfold the wings carefully. With all the extra cleaning I've been giving them lately, they look whiter than ever. He holds them delicately, as if they're the most precious things in the world.

"You can't give me these," he says.

"I just did." I nod at the wall behind him, calculating where all the picture hooks are. "Dad wants you to have them, too. I thought we could stick them up there."

I sit on his bed, smiling at the puzzled expression on his face.

"Dad's always said swans' wings are magical," I say. "I just keep thinking that if I give you these wings, you'll be safe. You know, safe for your transplant. Is that stupid?"

Harry keeps grinning. "You're amazing," he murmurs, his eyes never leaving mine. "Thank you."

He holds my hand to his chest and I can feel his heartbeat and his Hickman line at the same time. I think of someone else's bone marrow going in through that line, someone else making him strong. I just hope they do. He leans forward, and I think he's going to kiss me again. I shut my eyes, but Jack bursts into the room instead.

"I'm not waiting out there any longer," he says. Then, seeing what we were about to do, adds, "Sorry."

I leap off the bed and grab the flying model. Harry shuffles back into his pillows.

"This is Jack," I mumble. "My brother. I thought he could help."

I dig into my coat to get the string and masking tape I took from the kitchen drawer, and push them quickly into Jack's hand. Then I go over to Harry and help him out of bed.

"Sit on the chair," I say. "Jack and I will do it."

Jack stands on Harry's bedside table and I stand on the bed. Each of us holds a wing. We take down the painting of ships sailing on the ocean, and the other one of a cherry tree. We tie the wings to their hooks, then use masking tape to secure them more firmly. Somehow it works. The wings stretch out across the wall.

"I hope the nurses don't make you take them down," I say.

"I won't let them," Harry breathes. He keeps staring at me.

After a moment, I realize that Jack's still there, smirking at us.

"You're as bad as her," he says, laughing at Harry. "Birds of a feather. Isn't that what Dad says?"

He turns and slips out of the room. My heart beats faster as I hear the click from the door closing, and I lean toward Harry again. I brush my lips to his. I love the way his eyes widen with surprise as I do. I don't want to stop. I can't help thinking that this might be the last time we ever get to do this.

Harry pulls away, laughing breathlessly.

"Stay with me for a while," he says.

So I do. Neither of us talks much. We just look out the window at the lake. An unexpected beam of winter sunshine falls into the room, lighting up Harry's face and lighting up the wings, making them both shimmer. The sun is warm on my skin, and makes me think of spring. I hold Harry's hand tighter.

"I'll keep watching the swans," I say. "They'll still be there when you come out."

"*If,*" he says quietly. "*If* I do."

"You will. And when you do, we can go back to Granddad's lake again."

He smiles at that. The sunlight seeps into the room, making everything bright . . . the bedside table, the bed, the chair. The whole room is so filled with light. Harry's leaning back into his pillows, his eyes already starting to close.

Quietly, I get up to leave. When I turn to say good-bye, he's asleep. The wings spread out behind him, glowing. If I squint my eyes, they look as though they're attached to him. He's like a huge, bright angel, soaking in the sunlight to make him strong.

Something is whooping in my dreams. The swans are coming. They're flying quick and high, and there are so many of them. It's their long flight: their migration home. They're flying toward the moon. I'm standing outside, on the cold, damp grass, and I'm watching them.

There's a strange swan at the back. It's got wings, but it doesn't have a long neck. It's bigger than the others. But it's flying fast and confidently, as if it knows where it's going. There's a patch of green covering the bird's head. Granddad's hat! And then I realize, this bird isn't a bird at all. It's Harry. He's migrating with the swans, flying in their flock.

The swans start to disappear, fading into stars. They whoop again. And then, gently, their noises turn into a song.

A swan song. It's beautiful. As they fly into the darkness, their voices become faint. Only a low rumbling hiss remains. A sighing sound, like a person's last breath. But one voice is still clear. One small squawk of joy fills the sky.

And it startles me awake.

*T*here are tears on my face. I lie still for a moment, just breathing. In . . . out . . . in . . . out. I wait for the shadowy shapes in the room to make sense. There's a breeze shaking my bedroom window, rattling the pane like a bag of bones. I roll over and hold my knees to my chest.

"Harry," I whisper.

His transplant was today. I still haven't heard anything.

I sit up. There's a flapping noise, coming from outside. I go to the window, pull back the curtains, and look. I don't know what I'm expecting. Perhaps the swan from the lake. Or Harry, fallen from flight . . . fallen right out of my dream. But there's no one. Only the shed. The oak tree. The washing line. I watch a sheet move backward and forward with the wind, turning and flapping as if it's alive.

I lean my elbows on the sill. The night sky is clear as water. I scan my eyes across it, my head still full of my dream.

There are no swans there, no Harry. Just stars. For once I can see them through the fog of streetlights. I sigh into my hands and press my nose up to the glass. It had felt so real; it had felt as if Harry was migrating. Leaving me.

I shake my head firmly. It was a dream. It doesn't mean anything. My reflection becomes blurry as my breath hits the window. I wipe it. I stay there for a while, watching the moonlight threading through the trees and making patterns on the grass. Then I glance back up at the soundless, endless sky. Tonight is too early for migrating. The swans won't be leaving until spring. Even then they'll return. They always come back.

But Harry?

I climb back into bed and grab my phone from the bedside table. I take a breath and text:

Are you OK?

Then I scroll through my contacts until I get to Harry's name. It's four in the morning. Even if he's alive, he won't be awake, but I send it anyway. I don't even know if he can get messages in the isolation ward.

I lean back against the headboard and hug my knees again. The darkness settles around me, thick enough to smother. I don't know how long I sit there, just listening to the gentle creaks and groans of the house. The rattling against my window starts again, and I hear the flapping from the washing line. I breathe really, really lightly, as if I'm scared something might break. There's a fluttering that starts in my chest and works its way out into my body until I'm shaking all over. I don't take my eyes from the phone.

Then it lights up. I've got a message. I smack my head back into the headboard in shock and my breath comes out in a rush. I'm blinded for a moment by the sudden brightness. It's Harry's number. My eyes tear up as I read it.

I'm OK. I was just dreaming about you. x

ACKNOWLEDGMENTS

This book has been a very long flight in the making. In fact, it was originally called *The Long Flight* and began its journey several years ago during my MA at Bath Spa University. It's been rewritten ten times since then, its main character has changed gender, and we've lost and gained several characters along the way.

It would never have been possible without the brilliant "flock" of helpers around me. Thank you to so many people for their time and help with this book, and for the support, advice, and knowledge they've given.

My flock includes: everyone at Bath Spa University, most especially Julia Green, Mimi Thebo, and Richard Kerridge. Also Liz Wright, Philip Gross, Simon Read, Brian Christopher, Barbara Hughes, Linda Davis, Andy Daniell, Derek Niemann, Dr. Catherine Atkins, Daniel Burrows, Anna Bartlett, Lewis James, Cadi James, Cameron McCulloch, Susan Symonds, Hemanthi Wijewardene, Anthony and Bee Christopher, and all my Facebook buddies who helped answer research questions! And also Imogen Cooper and Barry Cunningham of Chicken House, Siobhán McGowan at Scholastic, and everyone on my publishing team.

A special thank-you to the bands Shearwater and Sigur Rós, whose uplifting, feathery albums kept me inspired through several all-night editing sessions!

This book would never have migrated without all of you.

Thank you.